Offsides

A Novel by

Erik E. Esckilsen

Houghton Mifflin Company Boston 2004

Walter Lorraine Books

Walter Lorraine @ Books

Copyright © 2004 by Erik E. Esckilsen

www.houghtonmifflinbooks.com

Library of Congress Cataloging-in-Publication Data

Esckilsen, Erik E.
  Offsides / Erik E. Esckilsen.
    p. cm.
  "Walter Lorraine Books."
  Summary: Tom Gray, a Mohawk Indian and star soccer player,
moves to a new high school and refuses to play for their Warriors
with their insulting mascot.
  ISBN 0-618-46284-8
  1. Mohawk Indians—Juvenile fiction. [1. Mohawk Indians—Fiction.
2. Indians of North America—New York (State)—Fiction. 3. Moving,
Household—Fiction. 4. High schools—Fiction. 5. Schools—Fiction.
6. Soccer—Fiction.] I. Title.
  PZ7.E7447Iro 2004
  [Fic]—dc22

                                                    2004000735

ISBN–13: 978-0-618-46284-1

Printed in the United States of America
QUM 10 9 8 7 6 5 4 3 2 1

For Lee—in his prime, a formidable fullback;
today, as ever, a champion brother.

Acknowledgments

The author is indebted to five Mohawk teenagers, students at Massena Central High School in upstate New York, for their valuable contributions to *Offsides:* Kristen Caldwell—Mohawk name, Katsitsienienh́:tha; Spencer Jacobs—Tehorihó:rens; Joanna Jock—Karakwinon; Sandra Smoke—Kanyenthah; and Kanentahawi Delisle Thompson. This novel benefits from their generous insights into Mohawk youth culture and into life, as they put it, on "da rez." Thanks also to Massena Central High School teacher Kathleen Dodge and Tom French, a teacher at Massena's J. W. Leary Junior High School, for making the "Mohawk roundtable" possible. West Coast teen reader Alana Miller provided useful feedback in the book's early stages. Finally, the publishing team—literary agent Wendy Schmalz and editor Walter Lorraine—kicked in hard, no pun intended.

Chapter 1

He stands alone in the silent, empty hallway. Only the sporadic clang of metal on metal echoing from the locker room undermines the illusion that he's the only person in the entire school building. He scans the trophy case, his eye drawn to a poster made from a blown-up *Southwind Sentinel* newspaper article. The poster is wedged in behind a row of trophies, like painted scenery in a school play. He wishes the article were imaginary, something to tear down and throw away when the pretending is all over. But it's not. It's real. A fact. History, recorded in a headline:

WARRIORS EDGE RAVENS 2–1 FOR SOCCER TITLE

And history is always written by the winners, he thinks, remembering his father's bitter words across the dinner table.

His eye travels to the subheading below the headline:

League-Leading Striker Held to One Goal

A photograph dominates the page: a huddle of dark uniforms, legs sticking out here and there, arms raised, index fingers aimed skyward.

To the left of the huddle, just a few yards away, he spots a lone figure in the visiting team's light colors. The player's jersey is untucked, his socks bunched around his ankles, his eyes cast downward. Enlarged to at least twenty times its original size, the grainy photograph reveals the solitary player's expression: a mixture of sadness and shock, as if he has just heard the worst news imaginable. In a way, he has—the referee's final whistle. Below the photo, a caption:

Southwind players celebrate their regional championship win Saturday. Tin River Union striker Tom Gray (at left) scored only one goal as the Warriors outlasted the Ravens.

Hearing footsteps approaching, Tom hitches his backpack onto his right shoulder and takes a deep breath.

"I'll tell you what," a man says, the stale odor of mint chewing gum drifting ahead of his squeaking steps. "I'm not sure even *I* would've put money on us that day." The man taps the showcase glass. "And after you scored on that direct kick, I had my doubts we'd be able to hold you."

"Well, you did, Mr. Dempsey," Tom says. "You held me to one goal. Some of your players *literally* held me."

Dempsey laughs and gnaws at his gum. "We play with intensity. That's why we're the Warriors."

Tom turns back to the trophy case, as if summoned by the Southwind Warriors' mascot. He regards the mascot's stern profile and furrowed brow; he traces with his eye the war paint streaking the figure's high cheekbone, the jet black hair flowing back from the flat ridge of forehead like a wave of anger.

Dempsey laughs again—falsely, it seems to Tom. "But you Ravens never quit," the man adds. "I give you and Coach Belden all the credit in the world for that." With a smile and a whiff of stale mint, he extends a hand.

As Tom's grip closes around Dempsey's, his eye travels to the SOUTHWIND ATHLETIC DEPT. patch stitched to the pocket of the man's maroon golf shirt—four upright arrowheads replacing the four *T*s, hunting bows the *D*s.

"So, Tom," Dempsey says in a softer, lower voice and scratches at his hockey puck–sized bald spot, which glows pink with sunburn inside a ring of close-cropped, red-gray hair. "Can I assume you're here for preseason training?"

Tom looks at Dempsey. The man's thin frame and slumped posture, his hands now stuffed in the pockets of his baggy khaki shorts, make him seem almost like a student killing time before class. "I'm not sure," Tom says.

Dempsey winces, as if Tom has just called him by his nickname among players throughout the league: "Coach Dumpster," itself an abbreviation of "Coach Dumpster Breath." The man hitches his shorts up onto his slight gut, clasps his pale hands behind his back, and begins rocking on his sneakers—black indoor-soccer shoes, which he wears without socks.

Feeling his heartbeat quicken, Tom turns away. He lets his eyes run down and back along the trophy case shelves, fixing his gaze on the silver bowl beside the newspaper poster.

Dempsey stops rocking. "Needless to say, Tom, you'd be a tremendous asset to our squad. There won't be a team in the league with our speed on the line."

Eyes still on the soccer trophy, Tom notices something

poking above the rim of the bowl.

"You'll play in the center, of course." Dempsey rests a finger on the glass. "I'll keep Plutakis at center midfield." He slides his finger down a few inches, leaving a trail of sweat. "I'll shift Young up from the midfield and over to the right wing." Dempsey's finger squeaks on the glass. "And there's a sophomore coming up, Malloy, with a good left foot. He can play the other wing. I'm also expecting this exchange student from England, a stopper or wing full, but I heard a rumor he smokes. We'll see what he brings to preseason. After today, he'll either be ready to kick the habit or kick field goals for the football team. If he hasn't got the lungs, they can have him, as far as I'm concerned. So, what kind of shape are you in, Tom?"

Despite the direct question, Tom continues to ignore Dempsey, stepping closer to examine the trophy.

"So, how does that strategy sound to you?" Dempsey pulls his hand away from the glass, steps back, and folds his arms across his chest. "I'd enjoy hearing your insights."

"What's that thing?" Tom says, flipping his chin toward the silver bowl.

"What?"

"Inside the trophy."

Dempsey leans forward, but in the reflection Tom sees the man look at him, not the trophy. He suspects Dempsey knows exactly what he's talking about. The object has a handle like a hammer, but thinner.

"Oh, that's just a memento of our championship season."

Tom leans closer to the glass, shielding his eyes to cut the glare. He notices a rawhide band wrapped around the handle. "Can you take it out, Coach?"

"Why?"

"Because I want to look at it."

"It's just a memento, Tom. You know, a souvenir."

"Take it out of the case, please."

Dempsey narrows his eyes again but doesn't budge. At the sound of voices echoing down the hall, he glances away, shifts his weight from one foot to the other, and finally relents: "Well, we shouldn't take too much time with this," he says with a blast of what sounds to Tom like nervous laughter. The man pulls a set of keys from his pocket.

Tom steps aside so the coach can unlock the trophy case and remove a tomahawk from the championship bowl. Dempsey leaves the glass door open as he hands the tomahawk to Tom. "There," he says. "That what you wanted?"

Tom runs his thumb along the blade, which is made of rubber. "No. I'd have no use for something like this."

"Coach!" someone calls from down the corridor.

Tom looks up to find Paul Marcotte, a Southwind wing fullback, passing by. "Tom Gray, excellent," Paul says. "We heard you're playing for Southwind. Dude, we're going to be unbeatable. Oh, Tom, man . . . sorry about your dad."

"Thanks," Tom says, noticing Paul's new purple-dyed hair and remembering his last match against Paul and the Warriors. Tom and the other Raven strikers easily beat him, a stocky kid with only fair speed, down the wing, but

Paul marked up as tightly on corner kicks as any defender in the league.

"You have a good summer, Marcotte?" Dempsey says.

"Great, Coach."

"Did you log some miles when you weren't in the beauty parlor? You ready to run?"

"Absolutely."

"Then run out to the equipment shed and get my chalkboard."

"Got it." Paul jogs the rest of the way down the hall.

"So, what's it going to be, Tom?" Dempsey says. "You with us or not?"

Tom turns back to the tomahawk. "Why was this in there, Coach?" he says, tapping at his palm with the blade.

"It's a souvenir, like I said. The Southwind Athletic Boosters taped them to a protein bar—you know, for energy—and gave one to every player before our match with you guys. For good luck. And, well . . ."—Dempsey chuckles, breathing mint-laced vapors into the stale air of the hallway—"you saw how well it worked."

"Yes," Tom says, feeling sweat rising along his hairline. He takes a couple of even breaths and looks up at Dempsey. "But I don't think it's funny."

"Try and look at it this way." Dempsey jams his hands in his pockets again and resumes rocking on his heels. "Playing on a team—playing on *my* team, anyway—is about putting aside personal issues and giving your best for the greater good."

"The greater good."

"That's right. The team, the fighting unit. Now, I know

6

about your father, and I'm just as sorry as a person can be about that. Honestly, I am." Dempsey looks away and scratches at his scalp again. "And I know about your mother's dissatisfaction with the school mascot. I've read her letters to the school board. Elizabeth Gray, right?"

Tom nods.

"In fact, I've been reading letters like hers for going on a year now."

Dempsey closes his eyes for a couple of seconds, and Tom thinks he detects a change in attitude, as if the anger, frustration, or whatever Dempsey has been holding back is starting to leak out.

"And I've heard all the politically correct arguments about why the Warriors' mascot is offensive . . .," Dempsey goes on, his voice a bit louder, and rougher, "and why we should change it, and why everyone would be better off if we called ourselves the Southwind Daffodils or Puppies or Tree Frogs. But I'll tell you what I think about all that." With one hand, Dempsey gestures down the hall in the general direction of the Southwind soccer pitch; he sweeps the other along the trophy case stretching nearly the entire length of the hallway. "What we have here at Southwind High is a tradition—a *winning* tradition. I don't think I need to tell you that."

Dempsey eyes the long, even rows of trophies for a moment, then begins walking toward the edge farthest from Tom. He stops at the first glass enclosure, about twenty feet away, and gazes at the awards. "This school building was built in 1966," he says, his voice echoing over the tapping of his fingernail against the case. "I was in that very first class." He rests his hands on his hips.

"We didn't even have a soccer team then. That wouldn't come until 1978. I know that because I was the first coach." He laughs to himself. "Not that I knew anything about soccer then. Not many people did around here. But we'd had winning teams long before the soccer program. Our winning tradition, the Warrior tradition, goes back to the very beginning. We've always been Warriors. And we've always been champions." Dempsey looks at Tom down the corridor. "Always, Tom."

After a few awkward, silent moments during which Tom just stares at the tomahawk in his hands, tempted to snap it in two, Coach Dempsey walks back up the hallway, his gaze never leaving the trophies—like the dictator of some small country inspecting his troops.

"What kind of teammate would I be if I let those guys down?" Dempsey says, drawing alongside Tom. "Especially the ones who aren't around anymore."

The man's tone has grown distant, Tom thinks, and even when Dempsey turns to him, he seems to look through him.

"Which guys?" Tom says.

"The Warriors I knew back then. And their coaches. And the community that made us a part of its history."

History.

"How do you know they'd be upset?" Tom asks, so tentatively that his voice cracks.

"Because *I* sure as hell would be," Dempsey snaps.

Tom flinches.

The coach seems a bit shaken by his own outburst. His soccer shoes squeak on the floor as he paces a few yards away and back again. "Let me tell you something, hotshot," he says, seething, that rough edge returned to his voice. "We did *not* fill this trophy case by letting people's petty, political complaints deter us from our mission. And we're not about to start now."

Tom takes another deep breath. "But why does the mascot have to be an Indian?" he says, scanning the newspaper poster. "There are other symbols of the competitive spirit."

With a sigh, Dempsey paces back down the hall a few steps. "Listen, Tom," he says, a bit more calmly. "Like I said, when I started coaching the Warriors, half the kids at this school didn't even know what soccer was. Same thing went for the community. But now everyone knows the game, and they know that Southwind's the best. We're regional champs, and it's not our first time." Dempsey stops pacing, crosses his arms for a second, then stuffs his hands in his pockets. "Look. What I'm saying is this: I know what it takes to build a team and keep it together. It takes four things: focus, focus, focus, and personal sacrifice."

Sacrifice. The word echoes down the hall, pulling Tom's thoughts away.

"He had once been an ironworker, and so he was always ready to help another ironworker. I'm one of those ironworkers, and I'll always remember how he sacrificed himself for his friends here at Kawehras, coming back day after day to help us with our troubles—troubles that Spencer Gray understood so well."

"Trust me," Dempsey says, stepping up to Tom. "You

9

put on the Warrior jersey, and I can guarantee you at least a couple of college scouts will come check out your game. The coach from State—Masseau. Guaranteed. And probably some others if you produce."

"My game." Tom half shuts his eyes to see the glints of light flashing off the awards. "It's just a game, isn't it?"

Dempsey snorts, bringing Tom's attention back to the man's face, now twisted in a pink sneer. "You actually believe that, Tom? It's just a game to you? Going to be a junior, already the best center striker in the league, and you're telling me it's just a game? So, in other words, you didn't listen to that radio interview you did before the playoffs last fall, didn't catch your highlights on TV after scoring that nice game winner at Burnsfield? Is that what you're telling me? Didn't read that full-page article about you in your paper up there, the . . ."

"The *Tin River Tribune*."

"Oh, so you *do* know what I'm talking about." Dempsey snorts again. "A game."

Tom looks down at his sneakers, new indoor-soccer shoes—Sambas—a going-away present from Coach Belden.

Dempsey raps his knuckles on the glass of the trophy case, rattling the sliding door. "Check out the hangdog look on this kid's face here."

Tom reluctantly looks at the *Sentinel* photograph again, his defeated posture, his downcast eyes.

"You put everything into that game, Tom. When we went up by one, you wouldn't let your spirit be broken. I watched you. I knew you were good, but you really earned my respect that day."

Broken. "What we ironworkers create is strong, but a man can be bent—broken, even. Spencer also knew this well, but he wouldn't be broken, and he wouldn't let us be broken."

"What does it matter what a team's called?" Tom says, trying on someone else's words. "If the game's so important, then what difference does a mascot make? Why not . . ." He stares at the angry Warrior profile in the trophy case, then shifts his attention to Dempsey's SOUTHWIND ATHLETIC DEPT. patch and, finally, to the man's face.

"Yes?"

"Why not compete under your own name, the name of your school, your town? Why hide behind this Indian head? That's not who you are."

Dempsey begins to respond but hesitates, stares at the floor as if counting to ten, the taut lines of his face twitching. "That, Tom," he says, "is either the worst attempt at reverse psychology or the steamiest pile of lefty political horse manure I've ever heard. No offense to your mother, which is where, I know, you've picked this all up."

"She's right," Tom says. He looks down the hallway, where a couple of guys are coming up the stairs from the lobby. "But leave her out of this."

"Leave Elizabeth Gray out of this?" Dempsey says. "I *wish* we could leave her out of this. What is she, like, a nurse?"

"Yes," Tom grumbles, his hands starting to shake. "But I told you to leave her—"

"An honorable profession."

Tom doesn't say anything, his pounding heart keeping

him from speaking the words spinning in his head: *Honorable. Yes, and honor is the reason I can't wear your red jersey.*

"Well, I'll say this much," Dempsey adds, sounding calmer. "She obviously takes good care of you. Maybe too good. Seems to me a time comes when a young man's got to start thinking for himself."

Tom looks away, but Dempsey steps into his view.

"What's it going to be, Tom? You ready to be a man about this?"

A man.

Tom turns to the newspaper poster again, his eye falling on the lone player sulking off toward the sidelines.

"If you did your best, son, then you have nothing to feel sorry about. Every player out there today—on both teams—respects you. They know you always play your hardest. I respect you too—as one hard-working man respects another."

Tom hands Dempsey the tomahawk. "A man doesn't play with toys," he says. Looking beyond the coach, he nods to a couple of Southwind players he recognizes from past matches. "You should move Marcotte to stopper," he adds. "He's too slow down the wing, and he's good in the air."

Dempsey grabs ahold of Tom's knapsack. "Hold up there, guys," he calls to his players. "Come on back here."

The players stop, turn around, and take a few tentative steps toward Dempsey and Tom.

"I want you to take a good look at Tom Gray."

Confused expressions on their faces, the Warriors look back and forth at each other, at their coach, and at Tom. Before Tom can move out of the way, Dempsey wraps an arm around him and presses him to his side.

"Here's what we call a hotshot," he says in the tone of a teacher explaining the most basic of concepts. "A guy who puts his own interests above the team's. In soccer, in battle, and in life, the hotshot's not going to be there when you need him. *Hotshot*'s just not a word in the Warrior language as we speak it. And neither is *quitter*— "

Tom slips from Dempsey's grasp and walks away. He resists the urge to run as the man's grating laugh dogs him, along with a phantom whiff of his stale-mint breath. Hearing the word *mother,* he spins toward Dempsey, but the coach is already herding his players into the locker room.

Tom looks at the trophy case. A black-and-white football team photo draws him in. The 1967 regional champions, the Warriors. He reads the names below the team photo, surprised to find "Brian Dempsey" in the caption. He scans the faces and finds the coach at the right edge of the group, looking much the same as a teenager as he does as an adult. In the photo he doesn't wear a uniform, just dark pants, street shoes, and a Warriors varsity jacket. He was the team manager.

Quitter, Tom says to himself. *Is that what I am?* He looks back up the empty hallway toward the locker room. He's alone again. *What just happened here? What have I done?*

13

Chapter 2

Tom sits on the bed in his new room. His backpack lies in a swath of sunlight illuminating clouds of dust around the boxes scattered on the sand-colored carpet. *Maybe I should get unpacked,* he thinks. *Maybe that'll give me something else to obsess about.*

The first box Tom lifts rattles with a metallic sound produced, to his knowledge, by only one object in the world. He sits back down on his bed, the box resting on his knees, and sweeps a hand across the sides and top. He picks at a red FRAGILE sticker, then tilts the box to read the words he scribbled on the sides the week before, back in his old room in Tin River: TOM'S TROPHIES—HANDLE WITH EXTREME CARE.

Last week, we were still in Tin River, he says to himself as he grabs a flap of packing tape along the box top and tugs at it. *In our old neighborhood. I was still a Raven. Now what am I?*

He removes from the box a plaque with one half of a miniature soccer ball, roughly the size of a tennis ball and made of hard plastic, glued to it. The brass plate beneath the ball reads, PLAY OF THE SEASON—TOM GRAY. He remembers the play vividly—the game winner, as it turned out, in the regional semifinal match against Burnsfield. More memorable even than the goal's bringing the Ravens victory—and a trip to the championship match with Southwind—was the kind of goal it was: a scissors kick from twenty yards out. Tom stares at a spot on the floor and replays the offensive push that led him to that pivotal patch of grass:

Fletcher's pass down the right sideline to Carr . . . Carr's long run to the right corner, where he heeled the ball back to Fletcher, who'd done the smart thing and followed Carr to support him . . . Fletcher's crossing pass from the right side of the field to a plot of empty turf just outside the line marking the top of the Burnsfield penalty area . . . Tom's sprinting to the space then, at the sight of the ball spinning through the rain, pacing his last few steps with the ball's descending arc, leaping off his right foot, cutting the air with the "scissor" of his left leg—

The sound of the front door opening interrupts the mental replay. That morning his mother told him she might come home from the hospital for lunch, but he knew that this was her way of saying that she'd come by to see what he'd decided to do about the soccer team. If he wasn't home, she'd know.

"Tom?" she calls. "You there?"

"Yes," he answers.

Silence seems to suck the air out of the muggy room. *Please don't come down here*, he thinks. *Please just leave me alone.*

"Hungry?" his mother calls—another question with a second meaning: *Do you want to talk about it?*

"No." He puts the plaque back in the box and sets the box on his bed. He reaches for his backpack.

A minute or so later, dressed for soccer but without his shin pads, he grabs his ball from the closet—still the only

15

thing in there besides the smell of fresh paint.

In the kitchen, he and his mother say nothing for a few moments as she eyes his soccer shorts and ratty Ravens practice jersey. "Hi, Tom," she says, seeming a bit perplexed by his uniform.

"Don't worry," he says. "I'm not playing for Southwind. I'm just going to that park we passed down the street."

His mother smiles and lets out a breath. In the next instant her eyes bend at the corners—sadly, it seems to Tom—and she takes his hand. "You know I support you no matter what, *owira'a,*" she says.

Tom resists a cringe at his mother's use of that word, *owira'a*—Mohawk for "baby," which is what he feels like every time she says it. But he'd rather be alone than complain right now, so he lets it slide and eyes the front door.

"You could change your mind right now and I wouldn't stop you," she goes on. "This is your decision. You know that, right?"

Tom nods, pulling his hand away.

"Do you want a ride to the park?"

"It's about three hundred yards away, Mom."

His mother looks down as if caught telling a lie, or at least trying to trick him. "Can we talk about this later . . . then?" she says in a small voice, leaning to look into her son's eyes. "I mean, I assume the coach, there—"

"Dempsey."

"He's not ready to deal with the mascot issue?"

"Not for me he isn't."

"Well, I'm sure he wouldn't do it for me either. Fortunately, we're not alone. Just this morning, I spoke to

16

the chairman of the Parents' Association. Apparently, some people are starting to come over to our side. Dempsey will have to change the mascot sooner or later. He thinks he can make this decision unilaterally just because he's a coach—"

"He's also the school athletic director."

"Right. I know that. But, still, when the people in favor of changing the mascot reach a critical mass . . ."

With a sigh, Tom steps toward the door.

His mother pauses. "You're okay?" she says.

Tom keeps looking away. "I'll be fine. I just need to get used to it, I guess."

"We will," his mother says in an upbeat tone as she moves to the sink and turns on the tap. "We'll both get used to it. Somehow."

August heat ripples above the brown-green grass in the park, empty except for a woman pushing two little kids on a swing set in a sunken play area just inside the park sign:

MILTON "SONNY" AUDETTE
MEMORIAL PARK

Tom had noticed the park when he and his mother pulled into town a few days earlier. It had reminded him, right away, of Tin River Park, down below the locks. He'd guessed, from the way the trees bent into a tunnel along the far edge of the park, that there was a river or creek hidden back there. So, before lacing up his cleats, he walks to the far edge of the park to check. Just as he

17

suspected, a creek roughly thirty feet across snakes into a dense forest leading back toward his condominium development.

He stares into the current for a few moments, enjoying the shade and imagining the creek winding all the way north to Tin River. He knows the two waterways aren't connected, but he indulges himself with the idea that the river could carry him home—and back in time.

Turning back to the park, he spots a kid walking into the center of the field. The kid carries a plastic bag in one hand and a board roughly one square yard under his other arm. He sets the board down and begins tossing items from the bag onto the grass. From where he's standing, Tom can't tell what the kid is unloading, but he thinks he sees wires sticking out of some of the objects.

Lacing up his cleats, he watches the kid assemble what soon resembles a three-foot-high rocket. Tom keeps watching as he stretches in the shade of the riverside trees. The moment he kicks his ball out into the glare, though, the kid turns to him and freezes.

Tom waves and, catching up to his ball, executes a perfect rainbow: His right foot rolls the ball up the back of his left shin, where it meets the flick of his left heel and arcs straight over his head. He settles the ball with his right instep and cradles it to the ground in the crook of his right instep and shin. *That's as good as I've ever done that,* he thinks. *How long before I lose my touch?*

"Soccer Guy!" the kid shouts, waving at Tom with what looks like a cell phone. "If you hear me scream 'Incoming!' make sure you duck." The kid lets out a slightly crazed-sounding cackle and begins punching numbers into the device.

"Where are you aiming that thing?" Tom calls back.

"Aiming?" The kid cackles again. "I wish."

Tom kicks the ball toward the kid, then juggles the rest of the way—knee to knee, knee to head, right foot, left foot, right foot . . . "I'll just stand near you," Tom says, reaching the launch pad. "That makes one less target."

"Smart thinking . . . for a jock."

Tom stares at the kid, a little tweaked by his tone: for such a scrawny guy, he's surprisingly lippy. His black buzzcut clings to his head like some strange, dark species of moss, and his pale skin seems not to have been exposed to much direct sunlight recently. His clothes—green corduroys, a white dress shirt with a button-down collar—further suggest that he doesn't get outside much. "Who said I was a jock?" Tom says, just to test him.

"You're not exactly dressed for a career in sales." The kid runs a wire out of a gray box just smaller than a car battery and clips it to the base of the rocket. "And I saw that rainbow. I may be the biggest geek you'll ever meet, but I know what it takes to do a rainbow like that."

"How do you know—"

"Stand back." The kid steers Tom behind him with his free hand and punches a button on the cell phone with the other. The kid glances around the park, settling his gaze on the two children playing a hundred yards away. "Hmm," he mutters. "These are not ideal launch conditions, but . . . hmm. Ah, whatever." He turns back to the rocket and punches more numbers into the phone.

19

"This seems dangerous," Tom says. "Are you sure it's safe?"

"Yes and no," the kid says with a shrug.

"What do you mean?"

"I mean, yes, it's dangerous. And, no, I'm not sure it's safe. But with so little wind, I think the odds are against hitting those targets down by the swings."

"Then why call them targets?"

The kid cackles again and, holding the phone up at eye level, punches another button. "Focus on the altimeter," he says, gesturing toward the launch pad.

Red numerals—a series of eights—suddenly illuminate a display screen the size of an alarm clock bolted to the board. "Commence countdown," the kid says as 00:25 appears on the screen. "Twenty-four, twenty-three, twenty-two," he counts.

At "zero," the battery clicks and a cloud of dense smoke forms around the rocket base. "Liftoff," the kid says, taking another step back and pulling Tom with him.

Just before the nose of the rocket disappears in smoke, Tom notices the orange fire gathering at the base. A split second later, the fire explodes with one quick pop—about as loud as a bike tire blowout—followed immediately by a *fwoom*. The rocket screeches into the sky.

As Tom watches the rocket rise, the kid quickly punches more numbers into his phone. "Ladies and gentlemen," he says in a smarmy, radio-deejay-style voice, "this is your captain, Preston Allard. On behalf of the entire crew, I'd like to welcome you aboard today's flight."

Tom turns to see the kid staring at the altimeter, which ticks off a rising string of numbers. Eventually, at just above 1200, the numbers begin to slow and then descend. "Not a bad launch," the kid says, "but the landing's the tricky part." As the numerals on the display screen descend rapidly, the kid punches numbers into his phone. "No," he groans. He punches the numbers in again. "Come on, open!" He tries again, but the numbers on the altimeter are now spinning downward so quickly that Tom can't read them.

Tom looks into the sky and notices the black form hurtling toward the ground. It looks like a duck that has just been shot, its wings drawn to its body, its beak rotating slowly. "I see it," he says.

"Well, take a good look."

A few seconds later, the rocket smashes into the field, erupting in a campfire-size flame. Tom reflexively jogs a few steps toward it, then stops. He turns to find the kid standing in the center of the launch pad and talking into his phone. "Allard Angel-Agitator launch log, August twenty-three," he says in his "This is your captain speaking" voice. "Model three. Model three launch—successful. Altitude—new altitude record established at twelve hundred, thirty-seven feet by measurement of base altimeter, recorded and stored in altimeter chip. Recovery and landing apparatus—total malfunction. Repeat, landing apparatus—total malfunction. Salvage effort to commence immediately. Prospects . . ." With the phone still to his mouth, the kid takes a small fire extinguisher from inside the plastic bag and walks to Tom's side. "Salvage prospects . . .," he repeats and holds the phone up to Tom.

"Bleak," Tom says.

With a cackle, the kid punches a button and stuffs the

phone into his pocket. "I'm Preston Allard," he says.

"Tom Gray." Tom shakes Preston's hand, and the two walk to the crash site. "I just moved here."

"From where?"

"Tin River. Up near the Canadian border."

"I know where it is. You live on the res?"

"No. In the village. But you shouldn't call Kawehras 'the res.'"

"Why not?"

"I don't know. I just don't like the way it sounds when you say it—"

"You don't live there. What do you care?"

"I used to live there."

"Why'd you move?"

"Long story. Anyway, that was before I started high school."

"So you went to Tin River Union?"

"Yeah."

"The Ravens."

"Right."

"Did you play lacrosse too?"

"Nah. For some reason, I suck at it."

"I guess you're not much of an Indian."

Tom nods at the fire. "I guess you're not much of a geek. But you've sure got a smart mouth."

Preston stares at Tom for a couple of seconds, then shrugs. "Sorry. Sometimes I get out of line. That's what they say, anyway. And, to be honest, I'm a little on edge at the moment." He peers at the melting rocket from different angles, as if he might learn something from the way it pulverized. "This is the third rocket I've trashed in five

22

days." Finally, with one extended blast from the fire extinguisher, he puts the small blaze out.

As Preston picks through the wreckage, Tom glances toward the swing set, where the woman has gathered the children to her side. "I always thought these rockets were just empty tubes," Tom says, "you know, once you launch them."

"Typically, they are," Preston says. "But I loaded fuel into afterburners on this one—rocket boosters, you know, to boost the altitude."

"Fuel. I can't imagine the cops would be too psyched about that."

"No, not really—ow!" Preston drops a piece of melted plastic onto the grass.

A copper-colored SUV with tinted windows pulls into the parking lot, its stereo speakers rumbling across the field.

"But, then," Preston adds, "the cops have bigger problems to deal with."

As Preston plucks plastic fragments from the grass and stacks them in his hand, Tom watches four guys walk from the vehicle over to a cluster of picnic tables tucked in the farthest corner of the park, at the end of the trees, where the creek disappears into the woods. "Are these bad guys?" Tom says.

"Not as bad as they think they are." Preston hands Tom a pile of warm rocket chips. "But they're definitely not Eagle Scouts." He gestures for Tom to follow him back to the launch pad, where Preston dumps the rocket fragments into the bag and indicates that Tom should do the same.

"What went wrong with your rocket?" Tom says.

"Signal problem with the recovery system."

"That's the landing system, right?"

"Theoretically. I thought I had it wired. Must be a code problem."

"It's a pretty sophisticated rig—or, rather, was."

"No, it just seems that way. It's actually a series of simple steps all strung together." Preston eyes the soccer ball. "Like that rainbow you did." Wiping his hands on his pants, he walks toward the ball and, two steps away, jogs into a rainbow maneuver. He gets the ball up onto the back of his left leg, but in his long pants he brings his left heel up too slowly. When he flicks the ball, it gets only as high as the back of his head. As the ball bounces away, he cackles and stumbles forward.

The guys sitting on the picnic tables hoot and applaud.

Tom notices one kid standing off to the side, smoking a cigarette. He's not laughing, just watching.

"How'd you learn to do a rainbow?" Tom says as Preston passes him the ball. He notes that Preston kicks with the side of his foot—correctly, not with the toe, as kids who don't know how to play soccer often do.

"You can see how well I learned."

"Did you ever play on a team?" Tom flicks the ball to Preston's chest, and the geek traps it and brings it down to his foot with notable control.

"I still do," Preston says. "Once a week, with a few other freaks. Two homeschooled kids and an exchange student from Sweden. Our parents basically make us do it."

"They make you play soccer?"

24

"They said we had to do something to get the rocket fuel out of our lungs."

"These other guys are into rockets?"

Preston kicks the ball ahead a few yards and tries to execute another rainbow. He's only marginally more successful this time. "Yeah, rockets are our thing these days. Rockets and greasy food."

"So, where are those guys?"

"They're probably at the Nucleus. It's a hobby shop down on Church Street. Geek central. There's a great diner next door—'great,' of course, being a relative term where diners are concerned."

Preston dribbles toward Tom, challenging him to stop him. Tom anticipates Preston's cut around his left side and easily plucks the ball away with the bottom of his left foot. Preston cackles, trips, and topples to the ground.

Tom turns to the picnic area again, where the one kid off to the side is still watching while the other guys sit facing in the opposite direction, toward the woods.

"But I'll tell you what," Preston says as he stands up and brushes grass from his pants. "There's no reason the others need to know about today's launch. Know what I mean?"

"How would they hear it from me? I don't even know them."

"No, but you'll meet them."

"I will?"

"I mean, you're going to kick it around with us, right?"

Preston dashes suddenly toward Tom, who lets him steal the ball from his foot. Even this effort nearly sends Preston tumbling over again.

"When did I say that?" Tom says.

"Well, if you're not playing for the school team, then we're the only game in town."

"How do you know I'm not playing for the school team?"

Preston chips the ball to Tom, who settles it with his right knee and lowers it to the ground in the crook of his right foot and shin. "Because their preseason training camp started today," Preston adds. "And I think you're developing an interest in rockets."

"Maybe. Never gave them much thought before." Tom executes another flawless rainbow. Dishing the ball off to Preston, he senses the kid in the picnic area still watching.

Preston tries another rainbow but fails more miserably than in his previous two attempts. "I give up," he grumbles, passing the ball back to Tom.

"You're not exactly dressed for soccer," Tom says. "I mean, it doesn't take a rocket scientist to figure that out."

"You know, that's sort of funny," Preston says. "Sort of." He picks up his launch pad and the bag of rocket trash. "Come to the Nucleus tomorrow morning, and I'll introduce you around. We'll get some breakfast next door."

"Okay."

"You like really fresh, healthy food?"

"Yeah. I guess."

"Well, we'll get some breakfast next door anyway." Preston cackles and hoists the bag over his shoulder like a maniacal Christmas elf and heads toward the street.

Chapter 3

The next morning, Tom catches a ride into Southwind village with his mother. He listens alternately to a super-amped-up radio show and his mother's plan to keep lobbying the school board to change the Warriors' mascot.

"Granted," she says, "'the Warriors' is a bit less inflammatory than other names, like those 'Red Raiders' downstate. They've got their silly Indian figure, the face with the war paint, the whole bit. Apparently, they even have a student who dresses up like an Indian and does a rain dance at halftime of their football games."

"Nice," Tom mutters.

"Yeah, the Warriors are mild by comparison, which is why the other parents and I have discussed keeping the Warriors name but changing the mascot to something less Lone Rangery."

"Lone Rangery?"

"You know what I mean. Indians aren't the only warriors, after all. You've got Vikings, medieval knights . . ."

"Good point."

"I'm glad *someone* thinks so. Right now it's the Parents' Association against the Southwind Athletic Boosters."

"Yeah, I've heard they have Boosters here."

"Bigtime."

"But they're against changing the name?"

"Bigtime."

"Huh." Tom remembers the Tin River Boosters, roughly fifty of the nicest parents he's ever met. They showed up religiously to Ravens home games and organized bus trips to some of the away matches. The boosters had been in full strength at Burnsfield when he scored on that scissors kick, which made him doubly happy, since they'd treated him like a rock star all season. After he was named all-division the year before, following his freshman season, they bought him a top-of-the-line equipment bag with his name stitched on it.

"But these boosters stand behind that coach," Tom's mother adds. "That coach you know so well."

"That I do." He wouldn't admit it to his mother, but Tom thinks Dempsey is more likely to resign than give in on the Warriors mascot controversy. Tom heard the man say it himself: *quitting* is not in his vocabulary.

"Where can I drop you off, hon?" his mother asks.

"Take me to the hospital with you. I'll walk from there. The store's just down the street, across from the library."

As they stop at a traffic light, Tom turns to his mother, catching a look with which he has become familiar in recent days. A distant look: out the kitchen window of their new place, on some spot on the living room wall as she looks up from the newspaper, at the dizzying blocks of technical jargon in the endless insurance paperwork they're both hoping will help them start their new life in Southwind.

"I'm sorry we couldn't stay in Tin River," she says with a sigh, "but this job here pays a lot more. And without any sure sign that, you know . . . with the insurance and everything still not . . . we simply need—"

"I understand."

Tom's mother turns to him. "Honest? You're okay?"

"I'm fine." He musters as much of a smile as he can without seeming to fake it. "But are you expecting this light to get any greener?"

His mother turns back to the road and lets her foot off the brake. "Wise guy," she says with a shake of her head.

Tom walks the quarter mile down Southwind's main drag, Church Street, until he reaches the library. Across the street he finds the Nucleus, wedged between a bridal shop and the Good Egg Diner in an ancient-looking building that forms a faded brownstone wall along one side of the block. The street reminds Tom of Tin River and some of the surrounding towns up north—the kind of Main Streets, U.S.A., that his father once told him were disappearing from the landscape.

The first thing Tom notices as he enters the Nucleus is the smell: the musty but strangely pleasant smell he remembers from his favorite shops back home—Buck's Hardware, North Country Sportsman, Tin River Toys. Standing just inside the doorway of the hobby shop, he wonders if the smell is the smell of time soaked into the worn, wooden floorboards and collected on the dusty lamps dangling from the high ceiling. Then he notices something else: the girl behind the cash register.

With her profile turned to him, he traces with his eyes the high rise of her cheekbones, the strong, angular line of her jaw. Her nose is small and round, not following the other contours of her face. Her satiny red shirt strains against her breasts as she works at a spot on the glass

29

countertop, the outline of her lean legs visible in tight-fitting, shin-length khakis. He estimates she stands about five foot three—short, solid, and strong. And pretty, in her own way.

He drifts closer, pretending to be looking for something along the shelves but stealing glances every other step.

A thin black headband holds the counter girl's blond hair back from her forehead, but a few strands arc over her blue eyes in one direction, over her tiny ears in another. A silver earring catches the light. A second later, the girl catches Tom staring.

"Are you looking at something?" she says.

Startled, Tom hesitates to answer. The girl's paralyzing gaze—like a sapphire stun gun—zaps an intelligent response before he can form one.

"Looking *for*," a familiar male voice answers from out of view. "We say looking *for* . . . when we haven't found what we're looking *for*." Preston and three other kids brush past Tom, Preston giving him a nudge in the arm. The three gather, smirking, around the counter. Two of the guys are red-haired identical twins of pudgy, pasty build. Even the freckles splashed on their chalk white faces seem identical. The other kid is about six feet tall and skinny, with a dishrag of black hair and thick glasses.

"We say looking *at* . . . when we can actually see it, whatever it is," Preston adds. "Does that make sense, Katya?" Preston gives the girl a cheesy smile.

She looks up into the fluorescent light, as if calculating. "Yes, I think so," she says with a nod.

"Let's try this exchange again," Preston says, gesturing for Katya to address Tom.

Katya smiles at him. "Good afternoon, sir," she begins in a formal voice, as if play-acting the role of a shopkeeper in a fancy jewelry store, not a hobby shop.

As she and Preston laugh, Tom mentally replays her accent: *"Good eff-ternoon . . ."* German? Russian? He also finds himself transfixed by her mouth—her full lips and the slightest gap between her front teeth. A film of sweat rises along his hairline. "Good afternoon," he says, not knowing what else to say.

"Are you looking *for* something?" she continues.

"Uh . . ." Tom turns to Preston for help, but the geek just shrugs. The other guys snicker under their breath.

"Katya, meet Tom Gray," Preston says. "He's the newest geek in town."

"Hi," Tom says. "I'm actually a soccer player."

"Soccer?" Katya says. "This shop doesn't sell soccer—"

"What Tom means to say," Preston cuts in, "is that he's joining me and the twins and Magnus for a little pickup soccer later on today. This morning, however, he's here to learn about rockets. Isn't that right, Tom?"

"Right," Tom says, relieved by Preston's motioning him away from the counter. "I'm interested in rockets."

"Sure you are," Preston says, leading him away. "And your first lesson begins right over here. See ya, Katya."

"Goodbye, English teacher," she says.

Preston whispers to Tom, "Say, 'Nice to meet you, Katya.'"

Tom turns around, but before he can speak, Katya flashes him another smile. That little gap in her teeth ties his tongue in a knot. He waves back instead.

"Smooth," Preston says as they turn down an aisle.

"She's kind of hot," Tom says when they're out of earshot. "You know, in a short-girl sort of way."

"Picky, aren't we?" Preston says. "For a new guy."

Preston and Tom catch up to the twins and the tall kid as they're scanning a row of boxes.

"Guys," Preston says, "Jock Man, here, thinks Katya's hot, in a short-girl sort of way."

The tall kid applauds. "Congratulations," he says in a deep voice. "You deserve the Nobel Prize for Obviousness."

"Right," one of the twins says. "She's beautiful like geysers give off steam." Both twins simultaneously let out an identically nasal laugh.

"Now, don't be snobs," Preston says. "Tom, these freaks are the McKinley twins, Alex and Stanley, products of a highly classified genetic experiment gone awry."

"Not true," Alex says and shakes Tom's hand.

"He got the looks," Stanley says, gesturing to his brother. "I got the brains."

"And this . . ."—Preston nods to the tall kid—"is Magnus Andersen. He's from Sweden. In fact, the word *Magnus* is Swedish for 'doorknob.'"

"Also a lie," Magnus says, shaking Tom's hand, "about my name. But it's true I'm from Sweden. My father is an engineer working here temporarily—"

"Fascinating," Preston interrupts. "The important thing to know about Magnus is that he has a car—a Volvo, naturally. So be nice to him."

"Definitely," Tom says. "So, what can you guys tell me about rockets?"

Preston and the others look at one another for a second

without speaking, as if Tom has said something stupid.

"I have a better idea," Magnus says. "Let's talk about rockets tomorrow. Today, we talk about Katya—over an omelet."

"I second the motion," Alex and Stanley say within a half second of each other.

Preston nods in the direction of the street. "To the diner, then."

As Tom follows Preston, Magnus, and the twins into the Good Egg Diner, he passes a booth full of Warrior-maroon T-shirts. As he and the others pile into the adjacent booth, he looks over to find Paul Marcotte cramming a piece of toast into his mouth with one hand and flipping his purple hair out of his eyes with the other. Paul gives him a nod.

Tom nods back.

He tries to focus on the rocket geeks' conversation—various and complex theories on the nature of Katya's hotness and what unlikely conditions would cause her to go out with one of them—but he's distracted by the murmuring from the next booth. He can tell Paul and his Warrior buddies are talking about him.

"Not that I would ever ask Katya out," Magnus says as Tom tunes back into the conversation.

"Why not?" Tom says.

"Because it might complicate my relationship with Mr. Gaz."

"Who's Mr. Gas?"

"Gaz," Preston corrects him. "Gazzayev. He's Katya's grandfather. He owns the shop, but you won't see him much. He stays in the back most of the time. There's an office and an apartment back there. It's where they live. But if you do see him, Katya'll probably be with him. He doesn't speak much English. Actually, none."

"Evidently, he was a successful scientist in his day," Magnus adds, "back during the Cold War. He's helping me with my latest rocket design, which even my father the genius cannot fully comprehend. But Mr. Gaz, he knows *exactly* what I'm trying to accomplish."

"So Katya's Russian," Tom says. "That explains the accent."

"It's sexy, isn't it—" Preston is distracted by a balled-up napkin sailing into their booth from the one behind theirs. "Excuse me," he says and slides out.

Tom instinctively slides out behind him.

"Hey, did one of you jock sausage-heads drop something?" Preston asks, holding up the napkin.

"Calm down, Einstein," one of the Warriors says—a beefy kid Tom thinks he remembers from last season. A fullback, probably not a starter. "That wasn't meant for you."

"Fact is, you filthy monkey," Preston says, seething, "it hit me—"

"So, here I am," Tom says. "If it's me you threw it at."

"Check this," the beefy kid says. "A geek and an Indian. I don't know whether to steal your notes or your land."

On reflex, Tom lunges for him, but Paul Marcotte, sitting at the end of the booth, stands and blocks his way. "Easy, Tom," he says. "Kyle didn't mean anything by it."

Kyle Erdmann. Tom remembers now: second-string sweeperback, took the Ravens' wing-half Marshall Kemp

34

out with an illegal slide tackle midseason last year. That ended up being Kemp's last game as a Raven. He was a senior.

"There's no trouble here," Paul adds in a tone that sounds to Tom as if he's really trying to prevent trouble. "Everyone, chill out."

Kyle slurps his milk shake and burps. "I'm surprised you'd even come over, Gray," he says and dredges up another burp. "Most quitters mind their own business."

"You might take a lesson, Kyle," Preston says and tosses the napkin at him.

Kyle catches the napkin. "You sure are a feisty little geek," he says. "If I weren't so stuffed, I'd kick your ass. I should've done it when you were at Southwind."

"You were afraid," Preston says. "And right to be. You've got a skull full of dog food, and you're not off my list yet."

With another burp, Kyle mutters "Psycho" and cocks his arm back as if to toss the napkin at Preston. Instead, he bounces it off the head of the kid sitting across from him—a player Tom doesn't recognize.

"Everything's cool, then," Paul says, nodding to Tom.

"Oh, very cool," Preston says with a sarcastic mini-cackle. "You just bring it when you're ready, Erdmann."

Kyle burps in response.

Tom and Preston return to their booth, and no one says anything. A few minutes later, Paul and his teammates get up. Kyle gives Preston, then Tom, a menacing smile.

"I mean," Preston says, nodding toward the Warriors now making their exit, "the guy burped at me. What am I supposed to say to that?"

"Are you some kind of secret martial arts expert?" Tom says. "Erdmann's kind of, well, big."

"Size and strength are not a universal defense," Preston says flatly as he scans the menu.

Magnus shakes his head and shoots Alex and Stanley an annoyed look.

The twins roll their eyes.

"What does it mean?" Tom says. "'Universal defense.'"

"You can't fight a kid like that on his terms," Preston says, eyes still fixed on the menu.

Magnus sighs and anxiously raps his spoon on his napkin, making a muffled knocking sound.

"And you can't let people walk all over you," Preston adds. "Especially guys like that—"

"Satisfied?" Magnus says, glaring at Preston.

Preston meets Magnus's gaze over the top of his menu but doesn't answer.

"Hang out with us long enough, Tom," Magnus says, "and he'll make sure you get killed."

"Western omelet." Preston sets his menu down and takes a sip of water. "The mind sleeps well at the inn of decision. Western omelet. Anyway, Tom, it seems like you and Kyle are the ones with the history."

"We do have a history, sort of," Tom says. He gazes out the front window toward the street. "We played against each other when I was at Tin River."

"Wait," Alex says, smacking his menu on the table, "you played soccer for Tin River?"

Tom nods, still staring out the window.

Stanley finishes the thought: "You're *that* Tom Gray?"

Tom turns back to the booth and locks eyes with

36

Preston, who's smirking a smirk that suggests he has a secret—or has been keeping one up to now.

"Stanley, how many Tom Grays do you think there are in this county?" Preston says. "I mean, think about it."

Stanley shrugs.

"I don't know," Alex says. "I've never thought about—"

"You two keep acting so stupid," Preston says, "and I'm going to have your parents arrested. Homeschooled, my butt. You're watching daytime television. It's turning your brains to home fries—"

"You're homeschooled too, dude," Stanley says with a nasal snort.

Tom turns to Preston. "I thought you went to Southwind, Rocket Boy."

Magnus sighs again, shaking his head.

"I used to go there," Preston says. "I'm homeschooled now, in addition to attending some other, shall I say, community programs."

Alex and Stanley snort under their breath.

Tom wonders about these "community programs," but just as he's about to ask Preston to explain, the waitress arrives. The promise of a hearty breakfast makes the question vanish on a whiff of fried food.

Chapter 4

They play three on two in Audette Park—the twins and Magnus against Tom and Preston—using their backpacks for goalposts. It's a more even match than Tom was expecting. In cleats and shorts, Preston turns out to be a fairly good ball handler. And although Alex and Stanley, in Tom's estimation, don't seem to understand the concept of supporting the player with the ball, always trying to give him an outlet pass, they have figured out the best way to get the ball to Magnus: in the air. Tom is surprised at Magnus's confidence with headers, despite his thick, tightly strapped safety glasses. In fact, the first couple of times he and Magnus compete for a head ball, Magnus makes the play.

Still, Tom knows he hasn't lost any of his touch. The ball sticks to his cleats like dog crap, as Coach Belden used to say, and he and Preston score more or less whenever he makes a run for the goal.

So he backs off a bit, doesn't go for the goal on every play but, rather, focuses on working Preston closer for a shot and on examining these guys' skills. The contest intensifies, tackles become more physical, and for a few moments Tom forgets that he's sharing the field with a bunch of science geeks.

As he moves around, he pays close attention to the way they build plays, move into empty space, and create opportunities to advance the ball. Their skills are uneven, and no one talks enough, but Preston and Magnus seem to grasp the basic architecture of the game, the sequencing of short passes to create openings for quick runs. As Preston jogs after a ball down in the swing set pit, Tom feels a familiar burn in the center of his chest—"the soccer fire," his father had called it. Today the sensation is welcome but also painful. As much fun as Tom's having with the geeks, they aren't the Ravens. And neither is he . . . anymore.

Jogging up from the pit, Preston gestures beyond Tom. "Who's this?" he says.

Tom turns to find a kid approaching from the picnic area. Tom recognizes him as the guy who'd been watching him and Preston a couple days earlier with that group of older-looking dudes from the copper-colored SUV. Tom looks toward the tables, but there's no one else there now.

"You guys need another player?" the kid says. He takes a drag on his cigarette and tosses his long, stringy, blond hair out of his face. He wears blue cargo pants, a baggy white T-shirt, and black boots.

"He's talking to you," Preston says, passing Tom the ball.

Tom turns back to the kid. He hasn't moved any closer, and he hasn't ground out his cigarette. He's clearly waiting for an answer. Tom chips the ball to him, an easy chip with a lot of backspin but not much velocity.

The kid surprises Tom by bending his right knee over the ball, letting it ricochet between the ground and his shin—a shin trap. Not that easy.

"Looks like he's played this game before," Magnus says.

"We can even up the sides," the kid says, knocking the ball back to Tom with the outside of his boot, putting a nice inside spin on it.

"All right," Tom says. "You play with me and Preston, but watch the boots."

"Cool," the kid says, taking one last drag before flicking his cigarette to the ground. "Name's Jimmy." He exhales. "Jimmy Biggins."

"I'm Tom Gray." Tom passes the ball back, but Jimmy turns around suddenly at the sound of a car stereo thumping into the parking lot. The ball skitters off his leg.

"Tell you what," Jimmy says, his eyes fixed on the SUV pulling in. "I gotta bail." He turns back to Tom. "You guys playing tomorrow?"

The others nod, but tentatively. "We could," Tom says.

"Well, could we play somewhere else?" Jimmy's tone sounds a little anxious to Tom.

"Like where?" Tom says. "I'm not from around here." He turns to Preston, who's standing with his right foot resting on the ball, watching Jimmy through narrowed eyes.

"Are *you* from around here, Jimmy?" Preston asks.

Jimmy backpedals toward the lot. "Just moved here."

Preston watches Jimmy retreat, Jimmy's attention shifting back and forth from the players to the SUV. "The high school," Preston says. "The outfield of the baseball diamond."

"Cool," Jimmy says, turning toward the lot and pulling a pack of cigarettes from a pocket.

"You know where it is, dude?" Preston calls after him.

"I'll find it," Jimmy answers without looking back.

The others are silent as Jimmy walks away. Preston flicks the ball up to Magnus, who heads it down to Stanley, who traps it on his thigh and settles it with his foot.

"That's weird," Stanley says. "He just moved here, but he doesn't know where the high school is?"

"He must be homeschooled too," Alex says.

"I'm thinking home*less* is more like it," Preston says, lunging for the ball resting at Stanley's foot.

Chapter 5

Tom is relieved, as they pull into the Southwind High School lot in Magnus's black Volvo the next day, to find the soccer field empty. He was expecting to see Dempsey and his squad running their afternoon session. *Maybe they're in the shade somewhere doing chalk-talk,* Tom wonders as he and the geeks pile out of the car and onto the searing blacktop.

Insect buzz mixes with the distant growl of an industrial-strength lawnmower in the midday glare. Tom and the others walk along one goal line of the soccer field in the direction of an embankment sloping down to the baseball diamond. Tom is tempted to step onto the Warriors' pitch, to drop-kick his ball into the empty net just to hear the knots creak, but he resists. Still, after he and his new friends have walked a few steps down the bank, putting them at eye level with the soccer field behind them, he turns to inspect the playing surface. From this perspective, he appreciates what only a serious player—and a coach with a decent budget—would appreciate: that a perfect soccer pitch is not flat but gently crowned, the turf sloping down from the center in a shape more like a huge contact lens than a blanket of grass.

It's a field fit for champions, Tom thinks, fighting the urge to imagine himself at the center circle, waiting for the whistle.

Jimmy Biggins is already down on the baseball field

when they arrive. Leaning against the center-field fence and smoking a cigarette, he wears what looks to Tom like the same baggy white T-shirt and blue cargo pants he'd had on the day before. The only change in his attire is a pair of new-looking cleats—new but cheap. ShUSA, a crappy mall-store brand. Technically not real gear.

"What's cracking, freaks?" Jimmy says, giving them a chin flip and flicking his cigarette over the fence. "Home run." He jogs toward the ball Magnus rolls across the grass and executes a decent rainbow. He traps the ball into a dribbling run across the outfield.

Tom watches Jimmy run, noting the way he uses the inside and outside of his feet, occasionally pulling the ball around in a circle with the bottom of his cleats. A few turns later, Jimmy stops to catch his breath. *Great touch,* Tom thinks. *Terrible lungs.*

Jimmy turns away suddenly, toward the woods on the other side of the home-run fence. A column of runners emerges from the trees and follows the outfield perimeter.

From where he stands, Tom notices Paul Marcotte and Kyle Erdmann in the orderly line of Warriors. "Go!" the kid at the head of the line calls out, and the runner at the back of the pack sprints to the head. "Go!" the new leader calls, and the kid at the end of the line breaks into a sprint.

Magnus draws alongside Tom and watches the players scramble up the hillside. "I hear Dempsey basically runs them for the first few days," he says in his deep voice.

"I know this drill," Tom says, catching Paul's eye as the Warriors pass them and head for the embankment leading up to the soccer pitch. "Some coaches call it an Indian relay."

They play three on three—Jimmy, Stanley, and Magnus against Tom, Preston, and Alex. The game is loose, lacking much in the way of strategy, but Tom can tell that Jimmy has chosen to mark him primarily. And he does a fair job of it, although Tom discovers that Jimmy isn't as quick on defense as he is on offense. But, then, he never gives up on tackles if he can get a foot into the play. Physical contact seems to be the strongest part of his game.

But those aren't Jimmy's only strengths. From a distance, Tom watches him mark Magnus, noticing how quickly Jimmy figures out that trying to beat the Swede in the air is futile. Instead, he positions himself to vie for the ball when it comes off Magnus's head. What Jimmy lacks in speed he seems to make up for with a solid mental game.

His biggest weakness, though, is obvious, and it pretty much reduces him to a virtual spectator after about ten minutes of play: lung capacity.

During one break in the action, as Jimmy casually follows a ball that Preston has kicked over the center-field fence—Jimmy no doubt seizing the opportunity to catch his breath—Tom notices a familiar figure at the far end of the field, next to one of the team dugouts: Katya, standing beside an old man in a wheelchair.

"Getting a little sun, looks like," Preston says, pulling a water bottle from one of the backpacks and gesturing in Katya's direction.

"Is that Mr. Gaz?" Tom says. He notices the old man fumbling in his lap with something.

"Yup," Preston says. "He comes here sometimes to try out new models."

"Models?"

"Robots," Magnus says, catching the water bottle Preston tosses to him. "It's just a hobby for him now, but he likes to make toy robots. They're not much different than the toys you can buy in his store, but I guess a long time ago they were considered very advanced."

"Robots," Tom mutters, his eye drawn to something moving in the grass a few yards in front of Mr. Gaz's wheelchair.

"He made one a couple of weeks ago that simulated a bear crawling on all fours," Stanley says. "Katya said he'd spent hours watching tapes of old nature programs, trying to get the body motions just right."

"I think the bear's a Russian thing," Alex says.

Preston and Magnus shoot each other goofy looks.

"Even *I* know that," Tom says, turning at the sound of feet approaching from behind. "And to the Mohawk, it's a symbol of strength. *Okwari*—bear."

Expecting to see Jimmy finally dragging himself back into the outfield, Tom is surprised to find Coach Dempsey and six of his players, including Paul Marcotte, Kyle Erdmann, and Chaz "the Spaz" Dempsey—the coach's son—coming toward him. Tom locks eyes with Paul for a second before Paul looks away, seemingly embarrassed.

Preston steps out in front of his friends and right up to Dempsey. "We thought that since the baseball team isn't using this field," he says when the man is still about ten yards away, "that it'd be okay if we—"

"Oh, it's fine," Dempsey says, a smile slicing across his shiny pink face, his eyes hidden behind enormous, pilot-style sunglasses. "We thought we'd come and join you." Dempsey walks up to Tom and rests a hand on his shoulder. "Tom Gray," he says, a piece of grayish chewing gum bobbing like a worm inside his mouth. "I see you've found yourself a new team. And what a team it is."

As Dempsey's sunglasses scan the group, Jimmy returns with the ball. "Who's this guy?" Jimmy says to no one in particular and flips his chin at the coach.

The Spaz and another kid laugh out loud, but the coach stifles them with a slight turn of his head.

"I'm Coach Dempsey, and these are the Warriors. I take it you don't go to school here."

"Homeschooled," Jimmy says and rolls the ball up into the crook of his right foot.

The Spaz laughs again.

"You got a problem with that?" Jimmy snaps at him.

Coach Dempsey's red-gray eyebrows arch up on his sunburned forehead. "Now, guys, let's not bicker," he says in an even, diplomatic tone. "That's no way to deal with each other." He turns to Tom. "What would you say to a friendly scrimmage, though?"

Tom sees the rest of the Warrior team sitting on the embankment beyond Dempsey and the six players with him.

"Come on," Dempsey adds in a tone sounding to Tom like that of a kid trying to persuade him to do something he shouldn't. "There's nothing to lose, Tom. It's not like this would count for anything. It's not like you're a real team—"

"Sure, we'll take you on," Preston cuts in before Tom can say anything. He walks over to Jimmy, picks up the ball, and tosses it to Dempsey.

The coach catches the ball and flinches, as if he hadn't expected his challenge to be accepted.

"You want to play here or up on your zillion-dollar pitch, the hallowed ground?" Preston asks.

Dempsey, still seeming a bit off-balance, doesn't answer.

"We'll play down here," Preston answers for him. "Alex, Stanley, push the goals back twenty yards each."

The twins hesitate, glancing from Tom to Jimmy to Magnus, who shrugs. Shrugging back, they each jog toward a backpack goal.

"You wouldn't want to mix up the sides, would you?" Preston asks, fixing Dempsey with a smirk.

Dempsey begins to speak, but Preston cuts him off: "No, that wouldn't work, right?" He rips out one quick mad-scientist cackle. "Then you wouldn't know how amazing your team is—and how amazing you, their coach, are. The whole exercise would be pointless." He gestures over his shoulder with his thumb. "We'll defend this goal. You can kick off."

Dempsey turns to his players, who seem a bit stunned, as if their coach had promised them Popsicles instead of . . . a scrimmage with a bunch of geeks. "Well, you heard the man," Dempsey finally barks at them, and they jog into position.

The scrimmage is a disaster for Tom's team. With Dempsey patrolling the invisible sideline and calling out orders, his players string together passes with SWAT-team precision. They communicate in loud, clear voices about every offensive possibility—"You got me square!" "Here, up the wing!" "Cross the field"—and the slightest defensive threat—"Man on!" "From behind!"

Tom tries to encourage the same level of talk among his own players, especially when defenders suddenly swarm him out of nowhere as he's carrying the ball. Preston and Magnus become more vocal, but it doesn't seem to be second nature to them, as it clearly is to Dempsey's squad. The level of competition, in general, seems foreign to Tom's players—especially to the twins, who run aimlessly around the field, chasing the ball with no apparent sense of the larger playing space.

Double-teamed virtually every second of the scrimmage, Tom nevertheless succeeds in getting passes off to Jimmy, Magnus, and Preston. Again he notices among these three a basic understanding of the short pass–by–short pass design of an offensive push, as well as the game's critical spatial dimension—the importance of running *into* open space to *meet* the ball, not just running *to* the person who *has* the ball. A few times, Tom gestures wordlessly to Preston and Magnus to move in the direction he's nodding, and they beat defenders with this stealth technique.

Jimmy, however, begins to show signs of fatigue almost as soon as the match begins. This, along with the twins' confusion about where to run, creates gaping holes in the team's defense. Inside of ten minutes, Dempsey's Warriors have scored almost as many goals. They cover so much of the field so fluidly that, after one particularly humiliating abuse of Jimmy and Magnus's feeble defense, Jimmy purposely kicks the ball over the center-field fence just so he can chase after it. When he reaches the fence, he leans over it and pukes.

"Well, it looks like you've got an injury, Gray," Dempsey says, pointing to Jimmy.

His face burning, Tom looks down at his cleats.

Jimmy hurls again, more loudly than before, and Dempsey's players laugh.

"Now, the Swede's not terrible," Dempsey says. "But he's slow. But this Preston kid . . . I remember him from last year. Bad news. The twins just run—and nowhere in particular. And it seems you've recruited a juvenile delinquent. That's what I'm seeing. That's your soccer team, Tom."

Tom glances up the embankment, where Dempsey's other players are laughing at Jimmy, who's still puking his guts out. He looks back at Magnus, Preston, and the twins standing in a loose huddle, grass-stained, beaten— but standing. "They're not so bad," he says.

"Don't get me wrong." Dempsey's tone has become a degree friendlier as he scratches at his bald spot. "I can actually understand where you're coming from on this school mascot thing," he continues.

"Oh, we're back to that."

"Come on, Tom. Work with me here. Our tradition here at Southwind is really bound up in that mascot."

Tom doesn't answer.

"When we see that mascot, we don't see something offensive."

"What do you see?"

Dempsey looks away then, toward his soccer field. "We see all the players who've come before, who've fought—

yes, fought for this school, this community."

Encouraged by Dempsey's slightly sentimental tone, Tom says what's on his mind: "I don't see that, Coach. I don't see any of those people in that silly Indian face."

Dempsey whirls back around, his mood clearly darkened. "No, I don't suppose you do," he says in a rougher voice. "A hotshot like you wouldn't." He looks at Preston and the other geeks. "So look at what you've got instead: a bunch of kids who don't even belong on the same field as the Warriors."

"We didn't ask you to come down here."

Dempsey clenches his jaw and clasps his hands behind his back. "You're talking to the athletic director, remember? What happens on these fields is my responsibility."

Blood pumping in his chest, Tom struggles to face Dempsey. "We've never played together before. We don't know each other as a unit, so we don't communicate very well."

Dempsey snorts. "If even one of those kids is good enough for my JV squad, then I haven't learned a blessed thing in more than two decades of coaching this sport."

Speaking of JVs . . ., Tom thinks, watching Chaz the Spaz trying to do a rainbow off to the side. He seems not to understand the sequence of three events involved in the maneuver: the step over the ball, the roll up the shin, the flick of the heel. Tom can't think of a single other team in the league that would put the Spaz on its varsity roster, but as far as he knows, the coach's kid has never played a game in a junior varsity jersey.

"We couldn't finish plays," Tom says, looking away as he mentally reviews the extremely rare highlights of their scrimmage. "But we were definitely trying to make them. And these guys have never played at a competitive level. But that doesn't mean they can't improve."

Dempsey makes a noise, a faint grunt, as though he's on the verge of saying something—whatever is now playing across his hard stare. He looks at Tom for a long time without saying anything, occasionally shifting his attention to Tom's friends, his Warriors, the backpack goalposts, and the embankment behind him. "You know what, Tom?" he finally says. "You're right. These guys do have potential." He crosses his arms and rocks on his shoes. "They just need a chance to develop it. They need some . . . goal that will bring it out of them. Right?"

Tom is silent, and the longer Dempsey stares at him, the man's gum snapping like flies hitting a window, the more uncomfortable he feels. Tom looks toward his friends again, surprised to find them now gathered around Katya and Mr. Gaz's wheelchair, which she has pushed to the sidelines of their makeshift field. Tom wonders how long they've been watching. Katya catches his eye and, with a wave, begins walking toward him.

"I'll make you a deal, Tom," Dempsey says in a rough whisper. "I'll give you and your friends a chance to prove what you're made of. We'll play again."

Tom turns back to Dempsey.

"Sometime before the regular season starts, two weeks from now," Dempsey goes on, "we'll play another match, up on the nice turf."

Tom starts to interrupt, but seeing Katya drawing nearer makes him hesitate.

"If you win, I'll change the school mascot," Dempsey

51

says, poking Tom lightly in the chest. The man steps back and rests his hands on his hips, as if challenging Tom to deny him that right. "I can make that happen, you know . . . if I want to. I'm the AD—and the swing vote in this whole crazy, mixed-up mascot business—"

"So why don't you do it anyway? Why not change it—"

"But if you lose," Dempsey continues, "welcome to the Warriors . . . for the rest of your high school career."

Katya steps into Tom's field of vision suddenly, smiling that gap-toothed smile that, in the day or so he has known her, has made it difficult for him to string words together.

"You going to be a man about this?" Dempsey says, loud enough for Katya to hear. "A man would say yes. A boy would say no. Which is it going to be, Tom?"

Katya gives Tom a puzzled look.

Tom starts to speak but stops, struggling for words that might bring the conversation back to reality.

"I'll take that as a no," Dempsey says. "Guess you're not a Warrior after all."

Before Dempsey is two steps away, Tom blurts out, "Yes."

The coach stops, turns, and smiles. "Two weeks," he says. "Oh, and by the way, I'll allow you to use the baseball field if you like. In the future, though, please get my permission beforehand."

Watching Dempsey return to his field, Tom feels his stomach clench like a fist, his head spinning. He wonders if he's experiencing a bout of dehydration, the effects of the intense workout he has just endured, or Katya's presence at his side. *Maybe all of the above*, he thinks.

"My grandfather," Katya says, "he watched your game."

Tom groans.

"He thinks you're a very good player."

"Thanks." Tom looks toward center field, where Jimmy leans against the home-run fence, wiping his mouth with his T-shirt.

"He wants to be your coach."

"What?" Tom turns to Mr. Gaz, who sits like a king in his wheelchair across the field, his royal geek-subjects gathered around him.

"He knows everything about soccer," Katya adds. "He's actually a soccer genius."

He's going to have to be a genius, Tom says to himself, *to make up for my stupidity.* Tom suddenly notices another man approaching from the sidelines, a tall, rail-thin man in khakis and an emerald green golf shirt—

Burnsfield High's color . . .

The man stops about twenty yards away, a clipboard under one arm, and watches him and Katya, as if waiting for an opportunity to speak. He seems to be in no hurry, but he definitely also seems to want a word with Tom.

Chapter 6

Stepping out of the shower, Tom hears his mother putting groceries away. He hopes she'll continue with her chore as he opens the door, a towel around his waist, and crosses behind her in the cramped condominium kitchen. She doesn't. She stops what she's doing and smiles. "Hi, Tom," she says. "How was your day?"

"Fine," he says, barely concealing a huff as he steps around her. "Do you mind if I get dressed before we talk?"

"Of course not." His mother turns back to the grocery bag on the counter.

Out of the corner of his eye, Tom catches a flash of nuclear orange as his mother stretches to place a box on a cupboard shelf. He stops, his eye drawn to the label: TastyTown Mac'n'Cheez.

Noticing him watching her, Tom's mother gives him a curious look. "Something the matter?"

Tightening his towel, Tom walks to the cupboard, reaches for the box, and sets it on the counter. Silently, he stares at it, his thoughts traveling back to the last time he saw this particular shade of orange, those wobbly letters.

"I have some chicken breasts thawing in the sink," his mother says, taking the box in her hand. "But if you'd rather have this—"

"Why'd you get this?" Tom says, taking the box back.

"Why? Because it's food, and in order to survive, human beings . . ." She studies him, a puzzled expression on her face. "Are you sure everything's okay—"

"I'm fine," he snaps. "Don't worry about me."

"Don't talk to me that way."

"Sorry."

His mother gives him a serious look. "What's on your mind, Tom?"

With a sigh, Tom stares out the window over the sink, losing himself in the hedgerow blocking his view of the neighboring units, his memory tugging him away.

He remembers the flavor of TastyTown Mac'n'Cheez, the way the cheese became like glue if he let his bowl sit for even a minute—if, say, on a Saturday visit to Kawehras with his father, his friend David Roundpoint led him out of the trailer to see a fox he'd spotted from the couch, where he and Tom ate lunch while their dads talked serious talk in the other room—sometimes shouting, sometimes laughing, often crying . . . Some of the grownups called David "Tawit"—*Dah-weet*—using the Mohawk pronunciation. Tawit's friends preferred the nickname "Skakenrahksen"—*Ska-ga-luck-son*—or One Bad Eye, for the way he'd squint one eye, cocking the eyebrow of the other, when he was suspicious of someone or something: a kid acting tougher than Skakenrahksen thought he really was; a teacher with a lame-sounding idea for a class project; shiny, unfamiliar trucks poking along the res roads, which usually meant that someone was in for a surprise visit from the Royal Canadian Mounted Police, the feds, the border patrol, the state troopers, or all of the above.

"You don't like macaroni and cheese?" Tom's mother says. "Or you *do* like it? Tom, speak to me."

"No," he says.

"No, what?"

"No, I don't want macaroni and cheese."

Tom's mother shakes her head, takes the box from the counter, and presses it into his bare chest. "Then please put it back for me. You're taller."

Tom slides the box onto the top shelf, pushing it way to the back, conscious of his mother watching him. "I don't like that kind," he says.

"How do you know? It's the first time I've . . ." Tom's mother halts in mid-sentence, glances up at the mouth of the cupboard where the box is now hidden. "I see." She turns and stares out the window too, as if also gazing back in time. "The kids at Kawehras eat this kind, don't they, Tom?"

Staring ahead, he nods.

"Well," she says with a sigh, "we need to cut a few corners ourselves now, at least for a little while."

Tom doesn't say anything.

"We'll get by," she adds, "but we'll make some sacrifices here and there—small ones, I hope."

Sacrifice. The word echoes around him, as if on the whisper of a ghost.

He turns to his mother and hitches up his towel again. "Did you hear from the insurance company?"

She clenches her jaw, looks into the sink, and takes a glass out of the dish drainer. With a quick shake of her head, she runs the faucet, one finger in the stream of water to check the temperature. "No," she sighs, filling her glass and holding it up to the light. "And we should probably try to stop thinking about it." She gulps the water down, as if to wash the matter away.

"That sucks," Tom says, taking one more look out the kitchen window. "They owe us that money."

"Yes," his mother says, setting her glass back in the dish drainer. "They do. But insurance companies spend millions of dollars on lawyers so they don't have to give anyone anything. Some people at the hospital are helping me sort through it, but we shouldn't get our hopes up."

Tom huffs and begins to speak, but his mother cuts him off with a look that requires no explanation—a direct look, chin raised slightly as if to aim her eyes more accurately at him. The look has long been a secret code in their family, and he anticipates the words before she even says them:

"It could be worse."

He fills in the rest of the sentence in his mind: "*We could be living on the res.*"

Chapter 7

Tom is awakened by a car horn honking just outside his window. Thinking it's someone picking up one of the three shrill twenty-something sisters who occupy the end unit of the neighboring condo block, he covers his head with his pillow, slipping back into sleep, the heavy summer air mixing with the mildewy odor of sweaty soccer gear in his room. The car honks two more times, then stops, but only a few moments later Tom is startled awake by what sounds like a dozen fists on the front door.

Rising, he pulls on the nearest articles of clothing—yesterday's soccer shorts and a faded Can Am Soccer Camp jersey—and walks down the hall.

Just as he reaches the living room and the door takes another volley of fists, it dawns on him that a few Warriors could be waiting on the doorstep, maybe to show him what they think of the Gray family position on their school mascot. He halts, crouches down, and retreats down the hallway, veering into his mother's empty room. Peering out her window, he's relieved to find a Volvo idling noisily in front of the carport, Magnus's spectacles flashing light in his direction.

"Get your stuff, Tom," Preston says the moment Tom opens the front door. "Gaz wants us down at the Nuke."

"Is the store even open yet?" Tom says through a yawn.

"Not yet." Preston shoves Alex into the bushes lining the front walkway. "But get your stuff anyway."

"What is he, the school principal or something? He snaps his fingers and you guys come running?"

Preston starts toward Magnus's car, turns, and back-pedals a few steps. "He's Katya's grandfather, dude!"

"Katya!" Magnus shouts through his open window and honks his horn once—a long, steady blast.

"You'd better hurry," Preston says. "It sounds like Magnus is finally ready to make his move."

Magnus honks the horn again—three quick toots.

By the time Tom and the others arrive at the Nucleus, Mr. Gazzayev, seated in his wheelchair and wearing a mustard-colored bowling shirt, is already directing Katya in setting up a chalkboard and easel. No sooner has she set the board on the easel than he barks something to her in Russian, gesturing wildly in the air with his papery, spotted hands. Wisps of silver-white hair swirl around his head like dandelion fuzz.

Katya disappears into the office and returns a moment later with a box of chalk, which she hands to Mr. Gaz.

The old man's blue eyes light up at the sight of Tom and the others, and he immediately begins tapping the chalk on the board and reeling out a string of Russian to Katya.

"Okay, listen up," she says with a firmness that catches Tom off-guard. She fixes Preston with a look that makes him, Tom, the twins, and Magnus all freeze. "He thinks that especially *you*," she says, pointing at Preston, "should listen very well."

As Katya pauses, one eyebrow arched like a bowstring, Tom catches the faint curl of her lip, a secret smile behind that stern mask.

"Because *you*," she fires at Preston again, "have the most to learn."

Katya turns to Mr. Gaz just in time to hide a smile from Preston and the others, but Tom sees the smirk.

She catches his eye and winks.

He manages, just barely, not to let his jaw fall open.

Mr. Gaz draws a big X on the chalkboard and says something to Katya.

"No more interruptions," she says and nods to her grandfather, with a sweep of her hand at the chalkboard.

Mr. Gaz's chalk-talk lasts about a half hour. Tom is impressed both with the old man's insight into the game and with Katya's ability to translate soccer concepts into solid English. At times, it seems almost as if she shares her grandfather's mind for the sport.

Eventually, though, customers begin trickling into the store, pulling Katya away from the chalkboard and leaving Mr. Gaz to speak to Tom and the others in Russian, which he seems willing to do, even though no one can understand a word he's saying. Eventually, Katya crouches next to his wheelchair and says something in a tone suggesting that today's session is over. Mr. Gaz tucks the chalk into his pocket and wheels into the office.

As Tom watches Mr. Gaz retreat, he's puzzled to hear him still speaking, as if to someone back in the office, out of view. Tom listens carefully but hears no response, though he thinks he hears a sound like shuffling papers and a file cabinet drawer closing.

Katya, seeing that Preston and the others are still watching her intently, flaps her hands at them as if shooing mosquitoes. "Soccer class is finished," she says as a father and son pair approach the cash register.

"So, do you guys feel like kicking it around?" Tom says as he and the others drift toward the front door.

"We could, I suppose," Preston says, "although that would make, like, three days of exercise in one week."

"Is that a bad thing?" Tom says.

Preston shrugs. "I don't suppose it's a bad thing, necessarily. It's just not a . . . geek thing."

"If we're not careful, we might turn into jocks," Magnus says.

"Who knows, you might like it," Tom responds.

Preston shoots him a curious look, as if he's picking up on something pointed in Tom's questions. "Well, what do *you* want to do, Jock Man?" he says as the group steps out onto the sidewalk. "You want to lead us on a ten-mile run or something?"

"I think we should kick it around," Tom says. "Let's see if Mr. Gaz knows what he's talking about."

Preston continues giving Tom a suspicious eye. "You think so, do you?"

"Yeah. I do."

"Why—"

"Okay, here's the deal." Tom lets it out in one burst, as if he has been holding his breath all morning. "This man . . ."

"What man?" Preston says. "Wait. Let me guess." He snaps his fingers and gestures down Church Street. "The yesterday man? At Southwind? Guy with the clipboard?"

"Right," Tom says. "Him."

"Who's the yesterday man?" Magnus says.

"A coach." Tom slumps onto the bench in front of the

Good Egg. "This coach from Burnsfield. Name's Mecklenberg. Apparently, he was spying on the Warriors, and he saw our scrimmage."

"You mean our annihilation," Alex chimes in.

"Can you spell that, Alex?" Preston asks.

"Um, I think so. Let's see: A . . . N . . . A—"

Preston cuts him off with an imitation of a game show buzzer. "Wrong," he says. "So shut it for a little while, okay?" He turns back to Tom. "Go on. Burnsfield."

"Right." Tom gazes down the street, struck once again at how similar this place looks to Tin River—from a certain angle. "He wants to play us, you know, for fun."

"Fun for who?" Stanley says.

"Fun for *whom*," Preston corrects him. "And that's it. Stanley and Alex, I'm telling your parents to hold you back a grade."

"Hey," Magnus interjects, "I'd rather stay back a grade than play another team like the Warriors. Why doesn't this Burnsfield team pick on someone else?"

"They're not allowed," Tom says. "They can't play other teams in the league during the preseason. So they're going to play us instead."

"They *are* going to play us?" Magnus kind of squawks, his deep voice cracking as it rises in volume. "You mean, you already told that guy we'd . . ."

"It won't be that bad, Magnus," Tom offers lamely, as if talking to himself. "I think they'll be cool about it."

Preston shakes his head at Tom and cackles. "Oh, where did we *get* this guy?" he says to no one in particular. "I mean, what is Jock Man, like, *thinking?*"

Chapter 8

Katya translates a running commentary from Mr. Gaz as Tom and the others cross the Burnsfield track.

Tom spots Coach Mecklenberg standing in the center of the infield, addressing his players, who sit in a cluster on the ground in front of him.

"You must remember, short passes are the only way," Katya says as she pushes her grandfather along the track while Tom and the others step onto the soccer pitch. "If you can move the ball around, you can control the speed of the game and create chances."

Mr. Gaz says something else, and Tom turns to him— but mainly to steal another glance of Katya pushing the wheelchair with wire-tight arms, her leg muscles flexing below crisp denim shorts, her pale forehead and cheekbones glistening with a film of sweat.

"And he says that because of you, Smoking Guy," she adds, "the rest will have to get back on defense faster."

"Don't worry about me," Jimmy grumbles. "I can hold my own."

"Yeah, we saw you hold your own all over the grass at Southwind," Preston says.

"The twins also have to support the player with the ball!" Katya calls a few moments later, seemingly an afterthought. "Don't always run away if someone has the ball. Run near him, help him. Short passes."

Tom catches Katya's eye. He's puzzled at the remark about the twins, which didn't seem to have originated with Mr. Gaz—not that Tom trusts his Russian translation skills.

Mecklenberg calls his name. When Tom turns in the coach's direction, he finds the Burnsfield Badgers on their feet and stretching, four players pulling the far goal in from the end of the field.

"We thought we'd go half field, since we're six on six," Mecklenberg says, extending a hand. "No point in giving ourselves a heart attack."

"I'm glad you think so," Tom says, shaking the man's hand. "But we don't have a keeper. Think we can use cones for goals instead?"

"Not a problem, Tom. Not a problem."

Unlike Coach Dempsey, Mecklenberg doesn't seem all that psyched that his team is clearly superior to Tom's. Although the Badgers score a goal every four or five minutes, their coach refuses to let them celebrate, instead commenting on the key things that led to the goal:

"See, that's what happens when you send the ball to the opposite side of the field . . . Nice communication up to the finish . . . Good, get in that habit of striking the ball one time, since you're almost never going to get a chance to tee it up all nice and neat. Just hit it."

At one point, Mecklenberg leads both teams in a quick offsides clinic, showing the fullbacks how they can move downfield like a unit to leave an offensive player behind their line—offsides if the ball is kicked to him, since an offensive player can't be closer to the goal line than the last defender, excluding the goalkeeper, when he receives a pass. Tom has known some players who were very good at breaking the offsides rule when the officiating of a match was loose, when the refs weren't paying close attention. *You just slip in behind enemy lines and quietly camp out until the ball comes your way,* he thinks. *And hope nobody notices what you're doing or makes a fuss about it.* Stanley and Alex seem especially perplexed but also very interested in the concept of offsides, leading Tom to wonder if there's maybe something in the geometry of the offsides rule—something about planes and points and lines—that appeals to their nonathletic interests. *Anything to get them thinking,* he says to himself. *Anything to keep them from just running around in circles.*

To Tom's surprise, Mecklenberg is also generous with compliments about Tom's team, giving Preston credit a couple of times for not bailing out on tackles—even against bigger players—and praising a smart run Jimmy makes down the sideline in anticipation of a head pass from Magnus.

Mecklenberg also praises Tom's play, but Tom more or less tunes him out as he analyzes his team's game for signs of improvement. When toward the end of the scrimmage Tom watches Alex drop in behind Magnus—taking up a clear supporting position—he slows to a jog. As Magnus, hearing Alex shout, "Behind you, Mag," flicks a heel pass back to Alex, Tom actually stops in his tracks. And when Alex, instead of trapping the ball, strikes it on the roll with his left foot—not even his strong foot—and splits the Badger cones, Tom almost drops to his knees.

The match ends with Jimmy puking off by himself again while Tom and the others shake hands with the Burnsfield squad. Mecklenberg gives Tom an especially strong handshake. "You know," the man says, holding Tom's hand a few extra seconds, "if you and your mom ever move to our district, you'll start as center striker—guaranteed."

"Thanks," Tom says, "but we're staying in Southwind for now."

"You made a tough decision not to play for Dempsey, there, Tom. I respect that."

"Thanks, Coach," Tom says, adding, to himself, *I doubt you'd respect the stupid bet I made with him later* . . .

Reaching their gear piled at the edge of the track, Tom and the others sprawl out on the grass. The sound of Mecklenberg jogging his team into the locker room mixes with the sound of peepers coming out in the marsh bordering the athletic fields, punctuated by the occasional heaving of Jimmy's stomach nearby. Tom stares into the sky, a gauzy blanket of dusk tinged with golden rays from the setting sun.

Suddenly, a shadow eclipses his vision. Katya looms over him, arms crossed. "You guys were much better today," she says.

"We got toasted," Tom says.

"Yes, but you improved in some areas. This is what my grandfather says." She extends a hand.

Tom's deadened limbs tingle with new life. He takes Katya's hand, and she yanks him to his feet. "In what areas?" he says, hoping to test his own observations against the old man's.

"Only a few," Katya says.

Mr. Gaz calls out to her.

As she turns around, Tom steals a full-on look at her solid, athletic body.

"Tom, I think my camera's in the car," Preston says, propping himself up on his elbows. "Do you want me to get it for you? Because a picture will last a lot longer."

As Magnus and the twins snicker, Katya turns back to Tom. "What's so funny?" she says.

"Nothing," Tom says. "They think I'm funny."

"You're funny?" Katya looks at the others, stopping at Preston, who nods his head.

"He is," Preston says, "once you get to know him."

"I don't understand," Katya says, narrowing her eyes at Tom, as if he's taking part in some joke—a joke on her.

"It's hard to explain," he says.

"Well, you can explain it in the car." Reaching into her pocket, she pulls out her car keys. "You come with us." She starts toward Mr. Gaz.

"Are you sure?" Tom says. "I'm all, like, pitted out." He realizes, a second after the words have left his mouth, how dorky he sounds.

"It's not my decision," Katya says without looking back. "My grandfather thinks you need more coaching."

Preston cackles into the grass.

On the way back to the store, Katya translates a stream of observations from Mr. Gaz, who gestures so animatedly from the back seat that Tom thinks he might snap his seat belt off. Tom is proud to hear his own observations echoed in the old man's notes, though he doesn't say so. There's something about the strong, forceful tone in Mr.

Gaz's voice, as well as in Katya's, that tells him he should just listen.

And that's fine with him. He's glad for a chance to sneak a look at Katya—the waning light glowing in her blue eyes as the sun shoots one last ray of brilliant orange over the treetops lining the country roads.

As the van crosses the Southwind town line, Katya tells Tom that she'll drop her grandfather off first. The words are like a shot of adrenaline pumped straight into his bloodstream. With Mr. Gaz back at the store, he and Katya will be alone.

Pulling into the lot behind the Nucleus, she asks him for help with the old man's wheelchair, but his legs won't let him move at first. Eventually he manages to give Katya a hand, although he suspects, from the confident manner in which she moves her grandfather around, that she doesn't really need his help. Or anyone's help.

While Katya's inside the store, Tom notices someone sitting on the loading dock at the end of the building block. From a distance and in the low light, he thinks the guy, partially hidden in the hood of a gray sweatshirt, is looking in his direction, but he's not positive.

Tom is startled by Katya yanking the back door closed, and he turns to watch her twist a key in the heavy-duty lock, then throw her shoulder against the door like a cop trying to bust into a criminal's apartment. Giving the door one last yank to test the bolt, she heads for the van. Tom turns back to the loading dock, but the Hood is gone.

"Are you waiting for me to open your door?" Katya says without a trace of humor, spinning the keys on her finger. "Let's go. I have much work to do tonight."

"Work?" Tom says, climbing into the van. "But the shop's closed."

Katya fires up the engine. "Yes, but that's when the real work begins. I must stock some new items."

"Neeew items," Tom repeats to himself, then reflexively grabs the sides of his seat as Katya punches the accelerator and aims the car at the mouth of a tiny brick alley. As the van shoots through the space and into the street, Tom looks to his right, spotting the Hood leaning against a building just around the corner, as if waiting for the van to leave. He and Tom lock eyes for a split second before Katya whips the car left toward Church Street.

"Hey, do you know this weird guy?" Tom says, turning to look through the van's back window.

"Most guys I know are weird," Katya says, her lip curling in that mischievous smirk.

As Katya pulls up to a stoplight, Tom sees the Hood duck into the alley. "This guy in a gray sweatshirt. He's been hanging around—"

"Yes," Katya cuts him off.

"Well, I just saw him—"

"Ignore him."

"But I think he might be planning to rob—"

"He's planning nothing, trust me. That's my brother."

"Your brother? Why's he lurking around like that?"

Katya pauses, sets her jaw, and adjusts the side-view mirror. "It's his choice," she says flatly. "He prefers not to be with people."

"Why not?"

Katya sighs in a way that tells Tom she'd like to drop the subject. "He works very hard. Even in a small shop, there's much work to do. He doesn't have time for people."

For a moment, Tom is tempted to ask Katya if she has time for people, as in *guy* people, but just imagining the cheesy words spilling out of his mouth makes him cringe. Fortunately, the stoplight changes, relieving the awkward tension that has been gathering in the van like steam in a locker room.

"Tell me where you live," Katya says, releasing the brake.

"The condos out by the water tower. Turn right—"

"I know where the water tower is." Katya flicks her directional signal and punches the accelerator again. The wheels squeal faintly as the van lunges into a turn.

"You drive differently when your grandfather's in the van, I've noticed," Tom says, his hand reflexively returning to the sides of his seat.

"Then maybe you'd like to ride in back?"

Tom and Katya are silent for most of the trip, and the longer they remain that way, the more difficult it is for Tom to think of something to say. He turns to Katya at one point, about to ask her what she thinks of Southwind High School, but he's intimidated by the very adult image she cuts against the backdrop of passing buildings—her eyes focused on the road ahead, one arm resting in the open window, the other hand casually gripping the steering wheel. There's a weight to her expression, a seriousness, that suggests she'd probably find his question boring or, worse, childish. He feels like a child in her presence.

"I appreciate the lift home," he says, just to say something.

"Why don't you play on the high school team?" Katya asks, as if this question has been occupying her thoughts all along.

Tom looks out his window. "It's complicated."

"You could be their best player. They're not very good."

"Thanks. They're regional champs."

"In Russia, they would lose to girls."

"They wanted me to play for them, but I decided not to."

"Why?"

Tom hesitates to answer, relieved to see the water tower rising on the horizon. "I had a disagreement with the coach."

"You are an Indian," Katya says, as if making him aware, in that slightly bossy way of hers, of something he has overlooked.

"That's right," he says, replaying in his mind the way her accent stretched the word into *"Eeen*-dian."

"Which kind of *Eeen*-dian?" she asks.

"Mohawk."

"And they . . . the school. They are also *Eeen*-dians."

Tom sighs. "Right. The Warriors. Like I said, it's complicated. Maybe when we have more time to . . ."

Katya slows down at the entrance to the condominium development, then accelerates suddenly, sailing past the driveway.

"You just passed . . . I live back . . ."

"So, you won't play for the team which is called like *Eeen*-dians," Katya says, again in that declarative tone, again seeming intent on explaining to Tom the details of his own life.

"Right," Tom says. "My mother doesn't think—"

"And what do you think?"

When Tom hesitates to answer, Katya shakes her head, as if disappointed.

"I agree with her," he finally says. "I told the coach I wouldn't play for him. It was my decision."

Tom figures he has given the right answer when, a moment later, Katya signals to turn into the Southwind Town Plaza shopping center lot, pulls around to the exit, and heads back in the direction of the condominiums.

"So," Katya says, "you have made your parents proud."

"I suppose. My mom's still trying to get the school to change the name."

"The *Eeen*-dians name."

"Right."

"And your father?"

Tom looks out the window again, realizing that they are not so close to the condos that he can stall for time. "My father died a few months ago." From the corner of his eye, he sees Katya turn to him.

"That's very sad," she says, signaling to turn into condo complex. "My parents also died. About one year ago."

"I'm sorry."

To Tom's relief, Katya actually makes the turn into the condo development on this pass. "We're the last unit on the left," he says.

Katya pulls the van into a space beside Tom's mother's car. She faces Tom, more or less expressionlessly. "They died in a car accident," she says without emotion, as if merely answering a question that she knows he would've asked her, if not now then later.

"Same with my dad," he says.

In the silence that follows, Tom doesn't know what to do. There seems to be more to the conversation, but he doesn't know what it is. Or maybe he's just supposed to say thanks and get out. He knows what he'd like to do, but he's almost positive Katya won't go for it. Just as he's about to reach for the door handle, Katya says, "You're a very good soccer player."

"Thank you. And you're . . ." As Tom hesitates, Katya smiles, exposing that little gap in her front teeth, a tiny flash of light from the carport flickering off her tongue. He leans toward her.

The moment Katya senses the move, she turns her head and throws the van into reverse.

Tom snaps back, blood lighting his face like a stove burner. "Thanks for the ride," he quickly says, opening the door and practically diving out.

"You're welcome," she answers without a trace of emotion.

Chapter 9

Tom is greeted at the door by the familiar smell of his mother's chili—that subtle, sweet hint of cumin swirling around the room like her signature written in the steam puffing from the pot on the stove. As he kicks off his Sambas inside the door, he's struck by how strongly the aroma of his mother's secret recipe connects him to home—their old home, back in Tin River. He's not completely surprised, then, to find his mother sitting in the living room, sobbing in the dark.

"Hey, Mom," he says from the edge of the kitchen light. He wonders how long she's been sitting there.

"Atonwa," she says with a heavy sigh.

The Mohawk pronunciation of his first name—*A-don-wa*—tells him that something is wrong. "You okay, Mom?" he says, stepping into the living room and sitting next to her on the ugly couch. The couch was included in the condo rental, its slipcover a tangle of green and orange vines against a cream background. Back in Tin River, Tom and his mother had agreed to sell the old furniture and start over in Southwind. They needed the money. Besides, there were too many painful memories of his father in those items they let go: the couch; the weathered plaid recliner; a nicer, forest green Naugahyde chair; the sturdy dining room table that Tom and his father had picked up at a yard sale coming home from Skakenrahksen's house one spring day when Tom and his friend were ten years old.

He misses that dining room table now, and he wonders if they also got rid of the musty blankets his father had kept in the trunk of his car in case of a winter breakdown. All of the ironworkers at Kawehras kept blankets in their cars, his father told him, since they often drove as far as New York City to work, and if a car broke down and one person had to walk for help, the other had to keep warm while watching over the car. Tom hadn't known those blankets were in there until the day they bought the table. He and his father used them to buffer its corners for the ride back to Tin River.

The blankets—there were two of them—would become a private joke between Tom and his dad. After a day visiting the reservation as a kid, Tom was often full of Mohawk pride, and when his father pulled out the blankets, rolled tightly like sleeping bags, Tom asked if they were Indian blankets. Or something handmade, maybe by Granny Brant or Skakenrahksen's aunt Wanda, the one who ran the Log Cabin restaurant and liked to decorate the place with Mohawk crafts.

"Oh, they're Indian blankets, all right," his father said, his wide smile catching the sun like a kite catching a breeze. "They came straight from Wal-Mart."

Looking around the condominium living room a second time, Tom is sure that starting over was the right choice. The old furniture would only look strange here, and that would only make adjusting harder. And those blankets had really come from Wal-Mart. Why would you save something like that?

His mother tucks his long hair behind each ear, a gesture from which he would like to recoil, but tonight he indulges her. "I heard from the insurance company," she says, her voice soft, as if she's easing him to sleep. She strokes the side of his face, then draws both hands to her eyes and breaks down.

Tom feels the urge to grab the cheap, included-with-the-rental flower vase from the included-with-the-rental coffee table and throw it all through the sliding-glass living room doors and onto the crappy, weed-ridden cement platform the rental agency calls a "patio." But as his mother uncovers her eyes and pulls him to her, wraps her arms around him, and buries her head in his shoulder, he realizes that the time for such reactions are behind him now.

"How could they say those things about him?" she cries, scratching him a little as her grip tightens. "After all he did!"

Tom catches their reflection in the screen of the included-with-the-rental TV—an Asian brand he has never heard of. The image of his mother clinging to him as if to a life raft, and of himself, head erect and peering about like a fox, sends a shock through his grass-stained arms.

She draws a choking, unsteady breath in between a free-flowing string of sobs, and he clenches her to him, his fingertips pressing into her soft back.

He imagines the TV screen now flashing the image of his mother hunched over, clearing his toys from their patch of lawn as storm clouds gather overhead; his mother hunched over his shoulder as he does his homework; his mother hunched over his father as the man—Spencer Gray, the brave man, the tired man, the angry man who

76

wanted to know, "How can a nation of people look at themselves in the mirror each day, knowing even the smallest detail of what our people have suffered?"—wrestled until the day he died with the temptation to stop off for a drink on the way home from Kawehras, on the way home from the homes he visited to help other men, his old ironworking friends, stay out of the Wolfclan Tavern. Skakenrahksen's home—and many more. This work was not his paying job at the underfunded, state-run drug and alcohol counseling service in Tin River but the work he did, free of charge, *after* his paying job.

"Kawehras—'the thunder.' In English, I say it translates as 'unpaid overtime.'"

Tom's mother cries for a while, and he holds her until she signals, with a little laugh, that she's finished . . . for now. "Thanks, Tom," she says, dabbing at her eyes. "I feel much better. You're my rock."

"So, the lawsuit's over then?" he says.

"This particular phase is, yes," his mother says, wiping her eyes. "But we can keep trying. It'll . . ." She catches herself, takes a deep breath, and nods again. "It'll take more time now, this next round of discussions. And there will be more paperwork, but there's still hope."

He sits in silence, not knowing what to say, perspiration rising on his forehead, temples, and hands, flashes of anger shooting through his body.

His mother sighs once more, dabs at her eyes, stands, and heads for the kitchen. "You had a couple of messages," she chirps, as if the scene in the living room never happened, as if he has just walked in the door and she's asking him how his day went. "Some man from Wittsford High School—Palmer . . . Paisano—"

"Palmisano."

"And your old pal Mr. Belden."

Belden. In the back of his mind, Tom has anticipated that Coach Belden would call to check up on him, but in light of all that has happened over the past week, he wonders where he'd even begin to tell the story of his clash with Dempsey—his clash and, now, his stupid bet with the man.

"They both said something about setting up a scrimmage," his mother adds as she removes the lid from the simmering chili pot. "Do they mean, like, with you and your friends from the toy store?"

Tom stares at his reflection in the TV screen again. The familiar smell of chili and the sound of his mother talking in the kitchen don't match up with his familiar silhouette against a strange background, the included-with-the-rental landscape painting hanging above the couch: two deer drinking from a brook. Back in Tin River, his father would've called to say he was on his way home. Tom scolds himself for not having shaken the feeling that his father might call, that he might return.

"That's right," he says, rising from the too squishy couch, his calves knotted and tight. "We're, like, a practice team," he says, limping toward his room. "We're a good morale booster."

His mother says something, but he can't quite hear it as he ducks into the bathroom, cranks the water on in the shower, then continues down the hall to his room.

Chapter 10

Tom rides in the van with Mr. Gaz and Katya, the others following as closely behind in Magnus's Volvo as they can, considering Katya's penchant for speed. Mr. Gaz falls asleep a couple miles outside of Southwind and begins snoring. "This is what my grandfather does on Sundays," Katya says. "If you put him in the middle of a crowd, and it's Sunday, he'll go to sleep."

"My father had a thing for Sunday naps too."

"It seems that many men do."

How did you get to be such an expert? Tom wonders, a jealous pang mixing with his breakfast and his frustration for letting his emotions tweak him, now, on a game day. He glances at Katya once, quickly. With her jaw set, her ice blue eyes fixed on the road, she reminds him of the osprey he and Skakenrahksen used to spot when fishing on Tin River: all business.

He stares out the window at the fields, the small towns he remembers passing through with his mother just a week or so earlier. He wonders how close they came to living in one of these towns—Frackville, Besser Falls, Molten—and not in Southwind. The thought cheers him up a little. Southwind's not so bad, and while he knows that pulling into Tin River is going to be hard, he also knows that things could've been worse—just like his parents had always told him. They knew this because things *had* been worse, when his father fell into his addictions—and then fell from that bridge job in Montreal.

"It knocked a whole lot of sense into me, Atonwa. Yessir. I didn't fall that far, luckily, but I'd been going down, waaay *down, for some time already."*

Tom glances back at Magnus's Volvo, which is following closely enough for Tom to see Alex reading a road atlas in the front seat; Preston pounding on Stanley's shoulder from his spot in the back seat, squished in between Stanley and Jimmy; and Jimmy with one hand sticking out the back window, a cigarette trailing smoke.

It could be worse, Tom says to himself. *I could be riding with those guys.*

Coach Belden greets Tom in the parking lot, gripping his hand and clasping the other onto his shoulder. "Welcome home, kid," he booms and stands back to regard Tom like some uncle who hasn't seen him in years—some tan, incredibly fit uncle.

"Thanks, Coach," Tom says, looking away quickly. That word—*home*—and the sight of the gigantic cartoon raven painted on the scoreboard at the far end of the soccer field cause a lump to form in his throat. "We'll throw our stuff over here," he adds, heading for the field.

"The hell you will," Belden says. "You're visitors, so you get the visitors' locker room. That's the Raven way. You know that—"

"That's okay, Coach," Tom responds, not turning

around completely. "We're fine here." He quickens his pace, takes another deep breath. He suspects that in the silence that follows, Belden and the others are shooting each other perplexed looks, but he doesn't care. He just knows that he can't go near the locker room, not without turning into a blubbering mess. Tossing his backpack onto the grass behind the near goal, he sits down.

"Well, all right, then," Belden says in an upbeat tone, which Tom takes to mean that the man understands the situation. The man always understood the situation. "Take your time getting warmed up," Belden adds. "We'll be out in fifteen."

The others toss their gear down. Katya wheels Mr. Gaz to a point along the perimeter of their encampment and begins translating the old man's instructions. The words wash over Tom with the faint breeze. All he hears is the rustle of leaves, which becomes, in his mind, the murmur of a crowd, which pulls his thoughts far away. His eye is drawn to the man he finds—and only he can see—standing at the near corner of the pitch, dark eyes wide with joy, one fist pumping the air victoriously.

The man smiles, opens his fist, waves, and disappears.

Tom stares at the ground until the tears retreat, and when he looks up again he spots Bill Miner and Sam Dodge walking toward him and Sean Fitzgerald—Tom's biology lab partner and last year's backup goalkeeper— just a few steps behind with a net full of soccer balls. *Why does it seem like I haven't seen these guys in years?* Tom wonders as he gets up and walks over to greet them.

Coach Belden jogs out a couple minutes later and blows

his whistle once, claps his hands a few times. "Okay, let's bring it in," he says, gesturing for both teams to gather around him.

As the players form a loose huddle, Tom watches Katya push Mr. Gaz's wheelchair toward the team benches, where the Ravens manager—a small kid Tom doesn't recognize—is meticulously lining up water bottles. As if this were the World Cup and not a meaningless scrimmage. *The Raven way.*

"What I thought we'd do is this," Belden begins, "seeing as Tom's team has a big match coming up . . ."

"What do you mean?" Tom blurts out. He hasn't told anyone about his secret bet with Dempsey, not even his mother—especially not her.

Belden shoots Tom a quizzical look. "Thursday night?" he says. "With Wittsford? At least that's what I heard."

"Oh," Tom says, trying to conceal his relief. "Yeah. Right. We're playing Wittsford."

Belden stares Tom down for a few seconds, as if giving him a chance to come clean.

Does he know? Tom wonders.

"Okay, seeing as Tom's so confident about Wittsford that he actually forgot about it," Belden goes on, "I thought we'd do some drills together first, get to know each other. Bill, Sam, and Sean, set up some squares for that Seventh Heaven drill. Looks like we should have three groups of seven. Go to it, please."

The players break up, but as Tom starts to gather with one group, Belden pulls him aside. "I need a word with you," he says, all the "welcome home" cheer gone from his voice.

Tom is almost positive now that Belden knows about his deal with Dempsey.

"Now, all I'm going to say is this," Belden begins. "Your decision not to play for Dempsey, in particular your reasons for not playing, are something you should be proud of. I can't tell you how much your old teammates here respect you for that. Now . . ."

Tom swallows hard, stares toward the scoreboard, where the angry super-raven glares at him.

". . . you may find this season tougher than you expected, watching from the sidelines and whatnot."

Tom nods.

"So, I want you to know that you can call me if there's anything you want to talk about. Call me if you're feeling down. Call me anytime you want. I'm thinking of trying to get to some state games this season, at least a couple. I'll take some of these jokers." He gestures toward the Ravens explaining the Seventh Heaven drill—a short-passing drill, one of Tom's favorites. "Maybe you'll come along with us."

"I'd like that, Coach," Tom says, relieved to find that Belden doesn't seem to know about the Dempsey match. His heart starts racing, though, as Belden turns to him with a very serious expression on his face.

"One big thing you've got to promise me," the man says, resting a hand on Tom's shoulder again. "You're not going to let Dempsey get to you. That's going to be the hard part, being right there in his school. Frankly, I question some of his coaching methods, to say nothing of the way he runs his athletic department. But I suppose I shouldn't judge." Coach Belden pulls his hand away. "The guy's a product of his environment, same as the rest of us."

"What do you mean?"

"Ah, nothing, really. It's just that I think his military experience, ancient history or not, sometimes finds its way into his coaching, and not necessarily for the better. He's a pretty good guy, but he can be . . . rigid. I mean, this mascot deal should've been sorted out by now."

"I didn't know he was in the military," Tom says.

"Well, it's not like he was career or anything. He did a few tours in Vietnam—volunteered, in fact. You don't meet a lot of people who can say that. At least, I haven't." Belden gazes across the field and shakes his head. "Dempsey," he says with a sigh, turning to Tom with a faint smile.

Tom takes solace in the man's familiar face, the gentle manner Coach Belden seemed to save for those moments—and Tom had experienced many of them as a Raven—when a kick in the ass wouldn't set things right again. When Tom had emerged as the player to watch around the league toward the end of his freshman year, some of the attention he received wasn't flattering. For every girl at Tin River Union who started saying hello to him in the hall, there was a dude who didn't seem to like the fact that the school's hottest athlete, at least as far as the local media were concerned, was a Mohawk.

Even some kids from Kawehras didn't seem to appreciate that one of their own was becoming so popular with everyone who was *not* one of their own. "You never talk about your roots," Skakenrahksen said the last time Tom saw him, just before the playoffs Tom's freshman season.

84

Tom had already done two interviews by then—one with the *Tin River Tribune* and one on the local public radio station. He and Skakenrahksen were drifting apart. Tom rarely accompanied his father on his visits to Kawehras anymore, not with Belden's weekend practice schedule and the rigors of high school academics. Skakenrahksen wasn't getting to school much himself, and he hung out mainly with older guys who'd gone to Tin River Union, dropped out, and moved on. They all smoked, drank, and drove around Kawehras in beat-up American cars. "Res rockets," they called those cars. Some of those guys had been involved in crime at Kawehras—smuggling cigarettes into Canada, where they could be sold tax-free on the black market. These kinds of problems had become more prevalent with Tom's generation and were some of the reasons his father, after he recovered from his accident, decided to move his family into Tin River.

Somehow, Belden seemed to understand that Tom's success on the soccer field wasn't one big, long hero's ride on everyone's shoulders. The coach understood well enough, at least, to respond in a way that kept Tom from going crazy: by not praising him too much during practices, not even on those days when Tom seemed touched by some weird soccer magic; by making sure he mentioned other strong players on his team whenever he spoke to local reporters; but mostly just by listening when Tom had to vent about the pressure.

Tom can already tell that it's going to be hard to say goodbye again, and the thought makes him look at the ground.

"You probably made a good choice with Dempsey,

Tom," Belden says. "I sure wouldn't want to play for him."

Probably, Tom says to himself. *I'm probably going to disappoint everybody before this is all over.*

Just as Belden had predicted it would, warming up with the unfamiliar Ravens players heightens the confidence that Preston, Jimmy, and the others bring to their game. Playing half-field but with no nets, just cones to mark the goals, Tom and his friends are out-hustled and out-passed, for sure, but by the end of the scrimmage, they've also scored three times to the Ravens' six. And, miracle of miracles, Jimmy doesn't puke his guts out when it's all over.

After the players have shaken hands, Coach Belden pulls Tom aside again. "That was a fine effort," he says. "You'll give Wittsford a contest if you play that well."

"Thanks. We do seem to be improving."

Belden cracks a smile. "I like your attitude, kid," he says, pulling Tom into a quick, firm hug. "Don't forget my offer. And don't be a stranger."

"I won't, Coach. Thanks. Have a great season."

As Belden heads for the locker room, Tom glances over to where his teammates are sprawled out on the grass—all but Preston, who's talking to some woman with a notepad. Tom walks back to their camp, and when he's about ten yards away from Preston and the reporter, he hears Preston say, "Name? Like, you mean our team name?"

Preston turns to him with a sarcastic smile. "The Boosters," he says. "We call ourselves the Boosters."

"Why Boosters?" the reporter says.

"You know, we boost morale." Preston smirks at Tom, who hangs back. "I can tell you, the Ravens are in a very good mood after playing us."

Alex walks over and nudges Preston out of the way. "But also, like, maybe . . . rocket boosters?"

The reporter gives him a curious look.

"We're into rockets," Stanley explains from a few yards away. "We're kind of, like, geeks . . . I guess you'd call us."

"But you've got Tom Gray on your team," the woman says, looking at him. "He's not a geek."

Tom avoids her gaze as he unlaces his cleats.

Preston lets out a mad-scientist cackle. "Tom Gray, not a geek?" he says. "Ms. Routly, you haven't done your homework."

As Katya pulls out of the school lot and aims the van down the River Road, Mr. Gaz's eyelids already drooping in the rearview mirror, Tom replays in his mind the questions Pamela Routly asked him during the sixty-second interview he gave her, mainly to find out whether she knew about the impending match with the Warriors. She didn't seem to have any clue about it, which made the exchange slightly less annoying. Slightly.

"Tom, is it true that you quit the Warriors because they wouldn't change the mascot name?"

"No. I was never on the Warriors to begin with."

"But what about the name? Your mother is supposedly leading the charge to have the name changed."

"Not exactly. A lot of people have been trying to get the name changed for a while. My mom's just another person who signed the petition."

"But Coach Dempsey won't go for it?"

"It's not entirely his decision to make, if I understand the situation correctly. He's the athletic director, true—"

"And the swing vote. In other words, he could change the mascot with his vote."

"So you do *know about this. Why are you asking me?"*

"Because, frankly, it's news when one of the best players in the league suddenly decides he's not playing soccer anymore."

"What was I playing today, croquet?"

Tom gazes out the window, his eyes lingering on the familiar scenery: the way Tin River pokes through the trees lining the roadside in sudden patches of deep blue, the railroad crossing just past the Wilson apple orchard, that ancient stone fence dividing that grassy field next to the half-knocked-down barn at the entrance to Kawehras.

Kawehras?

"Where are you going?" Tom says, snapping his head around to Katya.

She tightens her grip on the wheel and says nothing.

"We are *not* going—"

"I want to see it," she says. "And I'm the driver."

"I'll jump out, then." Tom grabs the door handle and flings the door open, turning to unbuckle his seat belt.

"Are you crazy?" Katya shouts, yanking the van onto the shoulder of the road.

She has hardly come to a stop when Tom leaps out of the vehicle, storms off a couple paces, turns, storms back, grabs his backpack off the passenger seat, and storms off again.

"Tom!" Katya calls.

Tom ignores Preston and the others as he passes Magnus's Volvo, which is pulled over about ten yards behind the van.

"Dude, what's the matter?" Preston says.

"Are we lost?" Alex asks, fumbling with the road atlas.

Tom walks, head down, along the side of the road, his heart racing, tears welling in his eyes. Everything about this place—the air, the smell, the light, even the sound of cars passing by—takes him back here. With his father.

Finally, at the sound of feet jogging up behind him, he turns to find Katya just a few yards back. He considers sprinting away, though he's not positive that he can outrun her. She's built for speed—and seems to like it. A couple of seconds later, she's walking alongside him.

"Tom," she says, out of breath, "what did I do?"

He glances over his shoulder in the direction of the reservation. He can see the reservation sign—

KAWEHRAS TERRITORY
SOVEREIGN MOHAWK COMMUNITY
WELCOMES YOU

"I don't want to go in there," he grumbles.

"Why?"

"I don't want to talk about it. I just don't want to. And if you're going in there, I'll walk from here."

"Back to Southwind?"

Tom turns and resumes walking.

Katya grabs his arm, and her warm, damp hand slows him down. "I'm sorry," she says. "I didn't know this would make you angry."

"Well, it does."

"I can see that." She holds his gaze for a few moments, neither of them saying anything. "I'm sorry," she repeats.

"No," he says, looking away, feeling the blood rush to his face. "I'm sorry. I just . . ." He looks at the Kawehras sign and shakes his head. "I have bad memories of this place."

"Okay," Katya says. "Then we won't go in there. Come back to the van. We'll go home."

She takes a few tentative steps toward the van, waiting for Tom to follow. As they pass the Volvo, Stanley pokes his head out the back window and says, "Tom, is this, like, where you used to live?"

"When I was a little kid," Tom says.

"Are we allowed on the reservation?" Stanley calls to him as he passes.

Tom turns and backpedals a few steps. "Sorry," he says, shaking his head. "Indians only."

"That's not true," Katya says as she and Tom climb back into the van, where Mr. Gaz is still fast asleep. "I asked that woman at the school, the reporter."

Tom eyes the old man in the rearview mirror. "Let's just go home."

They ride in silence for ten minutes or so, but as the route and landscape become less familiar to him, Tom begins explaining to Katya why he won't visit the reservation. "That's where my father was the night he died," Tom says, "driving on the res."

"Was he drunk?"

The question nearly knocks the wind out of him. Tom turns to Katya and stares, wondering if maybe he imagined her saying what he thinks she just said. "What kind of a question is that?" he hisses. His hands tremble for a moment as he fights back the urge to shout at her, to tell her what he really thinks of her blunt questions and bossy, know-it-all attitude. *What would you say?* he rants to himself, watching the telephone poles click by, *if I told you, yeah, the men my father had been driving home from the Wolfclan Tavern were drunk? My father, however, was stone sober—and had been for three years. And the man who crossed the center line and hit his car head-on? Not a Mohawk. Not another drunk Eeen-dian. But tell that to the insurance company. All they care about is the fact that there was alcohol and Eeen-dians at this crash site. And we all know what that must mean—never mind the police reports, never mind the autopsy or the eyewitness accounts, all of which say my father hadn't had a drop . . .*

Katya's sniffling interrupts Tom's private rant. He turns to find her wiping tears from her cheek with her left hand, her right index finger hooked around the bottom of the steering wheel. "My father . . .," she says, her eyes fixed on the road stretched before them, "he was drunk."

Chapter 11

Jimmy and Preston sit on the bench in front of the Good Egg, reading the *Southwind Sentinel*. Jimmy's smoking a cigarette, and even though the wind is blowing away from Preston, every once in a while the geek snaps the paper against his legs and glares at Jimmy for exhaling in his direction. Alex and Stanley lean against the diner's brick exterior, also reading the *Sentinel*. Only Magnus's legs are visible from underneath his car, which is parked along the curb behind Preston and Jimmy's bench. From where Tom sits, on the hood of the Volvo, he can see pages of the *Sentinel* scattered across the front seat. He read the paper at home over breakfast, and he wasn't thrilled about the news.

Pamela Routly wrote an extensive preview of the upcoming soccer season, including a sidebar about Tom's Boosters, which she described as *"a ragtag band of rovers with more tenacity than talent, but spirit to spare."* In the article she chronicled, more or less accurately, the team's progress over the past two weeks but didn't mention their upcoming match with Southwind—a sign, Tom figures, that Dempsey hasn't divulged their secret to the world yet. Routly did, however, note that *"former Tin River striker Tom Gray may have let youthful bravado get the better of him in refusing a starting spot on the championship squad.*" After reading the article, Tom unpacked his dictionary and looked up *bravado:* false bravery.

Though he'd been accused of similar things before, by Skakenrahksen and kids at Tin River who thought he needed to come down off the pedestal upon which the local press and Tin River Boosters had put him, he had never been criticized in such a public way before. It didn't occur to him, when he decided not to play for Dempsey back in front of the Southwind trophy case, that he'd have to answer for it in the newspaper. And what exactly did Pamela Routly know about why he made the decision he made? Nothing. What did anybody know about that, except maybe his mother?

Even Elizabeth Gray made the *Sentinel* that day, in an article about the Warrior mascot debate written by a reporter named Phil Olsen—"*with additional reporting by Pamela Routly.*" Tom got the impression, reading Olsen's article, that the paper supports Dempsey's position over that of the Parents' Association and his mother. Olsen gave Dempsey a long, eloquent quote:

> "*The Warrior tradition, as imperfect as it may be, has for decades brought our community together around a set of virtues—courage, perseverance, and the camaraderie forged in competitive athletics. Political debates such as this one have done nothing but divide us.*"

The article reported that Tom's mother was "*maintaining steady pressure on the school board to reconsider the team mascot—trying to head the Warriors off at the pass."* Tom suspected that this one phrase, *"head the Warriors off at the pass,"* had come from Routly, whose articles on the soccer season are all peppered with clever lines. Olsen gave his mother one short quote—*"The mascot denigrates Native American culture"*—and, in the process, gave Tom another word to look up. *Denigrate:* to attack the reputation of; to defame.

Tom is relieved that his bet with Dempsey is not mentioned in the paper, but even this bright spot, he knows, has its dark side: Unless Dempsey has forgotten about their wager or just decides to let the whole matter go—unlikely, given his comments in the mascot article—Routly's going to have a much bigger soccer story when the regular season finally starts. And she'll be proved right: Tom will be wearing Warriors red, his *bravado,* his false bravery, will have been just that. False.

"What do you make of all this, Jock Man?" Preston says, rolling up the paper and cramming it between slats in the bench.

Tom hesitates, hoping someone else will join the conversation. His thoughts on the matter seem too tangled to convey at the moment.

"Tom?" Preston persists.

"I hope you're planning to recycle that paper," Tom says.

Preston shoots him an annoyed look, but before he can respond, the group is distracted by Katya stepping out of the Nucleus. She stops in the middle of the sidewalk, puts her hands on her hips, and tilts her head back into the morning sun, closing her eyes. Tom fights the urge to stare and instead looks down at his Sambas, avoiding what he feels is just one more unpredictable factor complicating his already chaotic private life. A few moments later, he hears her walking toward them.

Tom looks up but in the opposite direction, away from Katya, just as the only person in the world more detrimental to his mental health rounds the corner at the end of the block: Dempsey.

Tom immediately hops off the Volvo and walks toward him.

"Where are you going?" Preston says.

Tom turns to find Katya standing at the perimeter of the gathering, hands on her hips again—but in a different way.

"Tom Gray," Dempsey calls from down the sidewalk. "Just the guy I'm looking for."

Tom turns away from his friends and hurries to catch Dempsey as far away from the others as possible.

"I heard this is your hangout," Dempsey says as Tom reaches him in front of the Village Florist.

Tom gestures to the shop. "Here?"

Dempsey laughs.

Tom smells the scent of stale mint gum.

"Here on the block," Dempsey says. "The diner, there."

"Right. Sure, I eat there once in a while."

Dempsey regards Tom with a smile and says nothing. He points at another bench in front of the store one shop farther up the block, a poster and framing store. "I just need a couple minutes of your time," he says. "Sit."

Sitting down on the bench, Tom decides to let Dempsey start things off. He's not sure he'd know where to begin anyway.

"So, Tom," Dempsey says, "you've probably read today's *Sentinel*."

"Yes."

"Well, then, you know that the reporter, there, Routly, managed to get in some information about your friends—"

"My team."

Dempsey laughs to himself and shifts on the bench. "Right," he says. "Your team."

Tom eyes the reflection of them, seated on the bench, in the poster shop's front window. Dempsey seems to be looking at their reflection too, as if it might be easier to talk to each other this way.

"Well, the problem with the article is not so much what she wrote. I think she got most of that right, actually. The problem is the way it makes our little . . . situation look. Do you follow me?"

Tom shakes his head.

Dempsey's reflection scratches at his bald spot. "It's like this." He turns to Tom, but Tom keeps staring straight ahead. "It creates a bit of an . . . image problem—for both of us, in fact. See what I'm saying?"

Tom turns to Dempsey. "Not really. I mean, I know I don't like being called a phony."

"What are you talking about?"

"Bravado. She wrote that I have bravado."

"Oh, that." Dempsey nods. "Yeah, sometimes these journalists are a bit reckless with their word choice. But, then, I'm no English teacher. I'm hardly one to judge—"

"It's strange to hear you say that," Tom interrupts before he's even sure what he's saying. "Because this whole debate is about word choice, isn't it? And aren't you making a kind of judgment about what one particular word means?"

Dempsey winces and gnaws at his gum.

"I mean," Tom goes on, "you sure seemed to know which words to choose when you spoke to that reporter, Olsen—"

"Look," Dempsey grumbles, his voice lower, rougher. "You want to get cute about this, Gray, then that's your choice. But I'll tell you how things stand, because you don't seem to get it. There are two things on the line here. One, you're going to look like a first-class jerk when you come slinking back to the Warrior bench."

Bench, Tom repeats to himself. The word is like a kick in the gut. "Did you say—"

"I sure did, hotshot," Dempsey answers on a big whiff of mint. "My team's a team. Everyone's equal. And if a player needs some time to sort that out, I know just where he can sit until he does."

Tom can't think of anything to say, his heart starting to pound in his rib cage at the image of himself dressed in a Warrior jersey and sitting on the bench wedged between Chaz the Spaz and Kyle Erdmann.

"I don't mean to be a hard-ass about this, Tom, I really don't," Dempsey says. He stands and walks over to the shop window, peers inside for a few seconds, then walks back to the bench. "I'm just trying to do the right thing."

"You said there were two things on the line," Tom says. "What's the other?"

Dempsey clasps his hands behind his back and rocks on his sneakers. "Right. I did. Well, the other thing is my own personal problem, I guess." He gazes down the street. "It's that I end up looking like the bad guy in all of this."

"What difference does it make how you look? You're the coach and the athletic director. You're in charge."

"Yes, but remember that I represent the Warriors, Tom—present and past. It won't do for me to cast that tradition in any but the most positive light—"

"So you put Chaz on the varsity roster?" Tom says, again the words leaping from his mouth by their own power. "When you know he belongs on the JV team?"

Dempsey scowls and folds his arms across his chest. "I'm through talking about this, Tom. Talking isn't getting anywhere with you. Here's the deal. I hear you're scrimmaging Wittsford tomorrow. True?"

Tom nods.

"I'll send one of my players out. Find him and tell him what you're going to do about all this."

"Do they know about our . . ."

"My team? No. No one knows. Just you and me. Not even that nosy reporter. But everyone's going to know sooner or later. The question is, are they going to know that you made a foolish bet and lost, or that you decided to become part of a very positive, very honorable tradition—"

"It's not my tradition any more than the Warrior image is your image," Tom blurts out.

Dempsey stares at him, eyes narrowed, for what seems to Tom like an hour. Finally, the man's expression softens, and he smiles. Without another word, he turns and heads back up the sidewalk.

Tom sits on the bench for a few minutes, staring at himself in the poster shop window, waiting for his heart to slow to a normal speed. He knows he's just been given an out, a way to save face and keep playing soccer at the most competitive level. He wants to give Dempsey credit for that. Something about the way the man deals with him, though, makes it nearly impossible to do anything but resist: the way he assumes his way is right, refuses to see another perspective, rejects any alternatives. And this business about riding the Warrior bench . . . That's the part of Dempsey Tom can't accept—the part that flips a switch inside and is suddenly nasty, willing to trick a kid into a can't-win scenario and to punish anyone who challenges his authority.

Yet Tom also knows that he's powerless against Dempsey. The man's been coaching longer than Tom's been alive—by a lot. The regional championship trophy is in a showcase down the hall from his team's locker room.

He stands and wanders up to the poster shop window, discovering that one of the three posters in the front display depicts a seemingly one-hundred-year-old Native American in full ceremonial regalia sitting astride a horse, the sun setting in purple-red hues in the background. The title running below the poster reads, SUNDOWN FOR THE WARRIOR. *I never had a chance,* Tom thinks.

Returning to his friends, he waves at Katya, who's taken his seat on Magnus's car. Without a wave back, she slides off and walks back to the store. Preston and the others turn and watch her leave.

"Want me to get my camera, Preston?" Tom says.

Preston turns around. "Dude, you totally dissed Katya."

"I didn't mean to."

"It sure seemed like it. Was it worth it, though? Did Mr. Coach Pants try to lure you back to the team?"

Tom hops back onto the Volvo. "Sort of."

"Did he offer you anything good?" Preston says. "A limo to school?"

"Not exactly."

"Well, are you going to play for the guy? Because that reporter made it sound like—"

"She doesn't know anything," Tom snaps.

His sharp tone silences Preston for a couple of seconds. "Well," Preston resumes, more delicately, "are you going to play for the Warriors?"

"Would it make any difference either way?" Tom says.

"See, that's just what I've been saying," Jimmy interjects.

Preston groans.

Jimmy drops his cigarette onto the sidewalk and grinds it out. "Does any of this make any difference? All this attention over a stupid game—"

"In this," Preston butts in, "I must admit, we're somewhat in agreement. But—"

"The only part I like is the thing about the Southwind Athletic Boosters," Jimmy continues, "you know, how they're pissed because we stole their name. The rest of this is fricking tweaked."

The group is silent as Jimmy lights another cigarette.

"And you, Tom?" Preston says. "Can you offer any insight more penetrating than 'this is fricking tweaked'?"

"See?" Jimmy sneers. "You guys are clueless. Bunch of

smart guys, geeks . . . but no clue. You think something like this actually matters?"

"I want to hear what Tom thinks," Preston says. "Does this matter, Tom?"

"Jimmy's right," Tom finally says, leaning back onto the warm hood of the car. "It's tweaked."

"No, but doesn't it say something about this community," Preston rambles on, now very amped about the issue, "you know, that maybe we put too much emphasis on athletics?"

"And not enough on science?" Magnus says, finally climbing out from under his car. "This sounds familiar."

"Seriously," Preston says. "Don't you think, Tom?" He walks over to the front of the car so he can look at Tom, who's lying down. "Doesn't this say something about what this community thinks is important? And what's not?"

"Yes," Tom says, straining to speak while on his back but reluctant to prop himself up and engage in this debate. "It says that it's important to debate things. And that it's *not* important to know when to shut up."

Magnus and the others laugh.

"You weren't talking about me just then," Preston says. He cocks his head to look more directly at Tom. "That wasn't a cut at me, was it?"

Tom closes his eyes and says nothing.

Chapter 12

The rain falls steadily all morning on the day of the Wittsford game but has almost stopped by late afternoon, when Tom and the others crowd around the front counter of the Nucleus for a chalk-talk from Mr. Gaz and Katya. As the two preside over the group, Tom can't help but think that the old man's coaching will be of no use this evening. At their best, the Boosters can string a few passes together, maybe score a goal or two. A strange, wet field is sure to screw them up.

He refrains from saying anything, though, instead focusing on Katya—her smooth arms, that little gap in her teeth. She has seemed distant this morning, but he refuses to let it get to him. He misjudged her interest once before; he's not about to assume that she felt slighted by him yesterday—or that she feels anything at all for him today. He's distracted, however, when he notices, through the space where the curtain doesn't quite block a view into the store's back office, a familiar form passing by: the Hood.

The Hood stares at Tom for a second, then continues on, out of view.

The chalk-talk must have been effective, Tom concludes as he piles into the back seat of the Volvo with Preston and the twins, because for once the Boosters talk about soccer the entire way to the match. Tom contributes a thought here and there, but for the most part he stays out of the conversation. For the first time since he met these guys, they actually seem to know something about soccer.

At the field, Tom approaches Coach Palmisano in the center circle. He's a shortish, completely bald man with a wrestler's wide frame and a mouth perpetually hanging open in an expression that seems uncomfortable and gleeful at the same time. They shake hands and agree to start as soon as the Boosters are ready to go, since the drizzle hasn't stopped, even though the early-evening sun is now rimming the treetops with a ribbon of gold. As Tom jogs back to his team, he spots Katya wheeling Mr. Gaz toward the sideline, both of them huddled under a neon yellow umbrella that she pins to a wheelchair handle with one hand as they move along. He's tempted to jog over and hold the umbrella for them. Catching Preston watching him, instead he walks to his gear bag and pulls out his water bottle. "Jimmy, do you have screw-ins?" Tom says, gesturing with the bottle at Jimmy's feet.

Jimmy ignores him.

"Seriously," Tom adds, "the grass is going to be slippery—"

"Well, I don't have fricking screw-ins," Jimmy barks.

Everyone falls silent. The mood up to that point had been fairly upbeat.

"Guy can't play a fricking game without spending a million fricking dollars," Jimmy mutters as he walks toward the field.

"I didn't mean . . ." Tom starts to speak but hesitates. He looks down at his own cleats—the top of the line. Mr. Coles, back at North Country Sportsman, gave them to him for free. There was a time, he thinks, when he probably could've scored an extra pair for Jimmy.

"Don't worry about it, Tom," Preston says. "It's not your fault he's poor."

"And he's been in a weird mood lately," Alex adds.

"Yeah," Stanley concurs. "The better we play, the crankier he seems. What's *that* about?"

Tom shrugs. "Let's just hope we don't get too good, or he might kill us."

"You know something, Jock Man?" Preston says. "The longer you hang out with us, the weirder you get."

By kickoff time, the drizzle has turned to rain again, the golden sunset covered by a nappy blanket of clouds. Except for Katya's yellow umbrella, the match seems to Tom like it's being played in black-and-white video. Even the pace of the game seems dull. Tom is surprised to discover that he and his teammates can actually string together passes along the slick grass—even adjusting for the sharper skip of the ball. He notices Jimmy trap a long cross-field pass from Magnus with particular deftness, especially given that he's not wearing wet-weather cleats. Still, they're unable to move the ball forward. They pass and run, pass and run, give up the ball, intercept the ball, pass and run, pass and run, give up the ball . . .

It's not until about fifteen minutes into the scrimmage when Tom realizes that, in all this passing and running and intercepting the ball, the Wittsford team hasn't scored yet. In fact, they haven't even come that close. Another minute later, as play stops for a ball kicked out of bounds, the rain intensifies, as if someone has just cranked a faucet a quarter turn. When play resumes, he hears it: the roar.

Tom has heard this roar before. In Burnsfield. The semifinal match he won for the Ravens with that spectacular scissors kick.

The semifinal match had begun in a drizzle, but by the half the rain was falling steadily. When the second half began, play was swallowed in a downpour—warm blobs of water large enough to smack when they hit Tom's neck and face. He felt like a horse dragging a plow across a field, every run, every move, demanding an extra push into the sodden ground, the water adding pounds, it seemed, to his uniform. At one point, looking toward the bleachers, he saw that the Tin River Boosters had risen to their feet. The crowd's cheering added a kind of white noise, like static, to the thump of cleats pounding the turf, the ball's sizzle as it sheared water and skipped across the grass. The ref's whistle could barely cut through it all—as faint and distant as a train leaving town. As Tom watched the ref jog to a spot about ten yards away from him and toss the ball to Garvey, he realized that he'd completely lost his grip on time. "Ravens throw-in," the ref called out, his voice like a whisper behind a waterfall. "We've got three minutes on the clock."

Tom had played the game of his life, and his body screamed it. He'd burned every last ounce of energy, picked up a huge welt on his left hip in a slide tackle, knocked heads with a fullback going up for the same corner kick, and even jammed a couple of fingers landing after a failed diving header. He was finished, done.

Later that night, discussing the game with his father over a celebratory pizza at the Tin River Grotto, Tom wondered if his exhausted state might have explained the bizarre experience that had begun with the Ravens' final offensive push, when Garvey threw the ball in to Fletcher . . . Fletcher made a pass down the right sideline to Carr . . .

"It was like time had stopped," he explained to his father. "I'd look at the sidelines, and people cheering would seem to be moving in slow motion. I'd look back to the field, and my eye would hit the ball like a hawk spotting a field mouse. It was like my blood had turned to pure adrenaline. And there was this strange . . . roar."

"You were in the zone, Tom," his father said, a knowing smile on his wide face. "Yes, I think you were."

"Have you ever been in the zone?"

His father laughed then—one of those open laughs, his head bent back, that told Tom that the man was remembering something. "Some people think this is what makes Mohawk ironworkers so good at what we do," he said, running one hand through his ink black hair, which was cut short but winged out at the sides in the humidity. With his other hand he rubbed the iron ring he wore on a rawhide lanyard around his neck—a gift from his old crew. "They think we spend all day in this . . . zone, where we're absolutely without fear."

"But you're afraid?"

"Certainly. When I was an ironworker, there were times when I was plenty afraid—just as your uncle Bo and Tawit's dad and all of them are. Anyone walking along a narrow beam so high up in the air is right to be afraid once in a while."

"What's the difference, then, between that and being in the zone?"

His father paused and stared out the window of the pizzeria. The rain ticked on cars in the parking lot like iron chips falling from the sky. "In the zone today, I think you were totally connected to what you were doing," he said. "Or maybe you were feeling very connected to your team. That's something I remember well from ironworking—we work very closely together. We depend on each other. And we get so we can communicate without even speaking sometimes." He smiled again, as if about to laugh. "This." He gestured with his head toward the parking lot.

"The rain?"

"No, the way we're always using our head to talk, you know, pointing with our chin at something or nodding. You do this too. Maybe you've forgotten, but this is the way people talk at Kawehras."

"It's a Mohawk thing?"

"More like an ironworker thing."

An image flashed in Tom's mind of his former best friend, Skakenrahksen, flipping his chin toward the door of his family's trailer as a conspicuously new-looking truck cruised past.

"Or maybe," Tom's father continued, "in those moments of being in the zone, you were all at once aware of everything having to do with that match—and aware of nothing not having to do with your match. You were aware of so many things that maybe time had to slow down for you to make room for all of them in your mind." He laughed again and shook his head. "Up on those beams, we're aware of everything also, including our fear. But mainly we know we're making good money for that work and that we're better ironworkers than the others, the ones who aren't Mohawks. That competitive instinct, Tom . . . the Kawehras ironworkers understand that well. We're known as the best, and so we work hard to remain the best." He cocked his head and looked away again, toward the rain-streaked window. "So we learn to live with the fear, since, up there, there's nowhere to escape from it." He winked at Tom. "Especially on breezy days."

"Maybe I knew I couldn't escape from the game," Tom said, wanting in that moment, more than at any other time he could remember, to know what his father had endured in his struggle—with ironwork, alcohol, failure, shame, and everything else that seemed to await him in his friends' homes at Kawehras after work almost every day. It had been about a year since Tom had been back there.

"Maybe I forgot how I was supposed to react to my fear of losing the match," Tom added, privately wondering if he knew anything at all about being a Mohawk anymore.

"Maybe," his father said. "You don't like to lose, that's for sure." He smiled. "But there are worse things than losing a soccer match. Think about losing your footing . . ." —he tilted his head back and looked into the ceiling— ". . . *waaay* up there."

Jimmy fakes a throw-in to Tom, which snaps him out of his daze. In the next instant, he watches Jimmy throw the ball to Magnus, who fields it off his head to Alex. Alex carries the ball across the field fifteen yards ahead of Tom and heel-passes back to him. As if playing in his sleep, Tom not so much fields the ball as *watches* himself field the ball, settling it with his right foot. He cocks his leg back to send a chip downfield to Stanley but hesitates as Stanley, noticing his own field position well behind the nearest defender in the Wittsford end, sprints back upfield to avoid being offsides. An instant later, Tom sends him the ball. Tom starts to follow his pass but hesitates as he observes—again, as if in a dream—Stanley faking a pass to Preston, who's standing in front of the Wittsford cones, then driving the ball just inside the right cone.

The Boosters have scored.

They are, in fact, winning.

For a few seconds, Tom and his teammates just look at one another, speechless. Stanley, still off-balance from his shot, stumbles a few steps and falls into what sounds, as his body hits the ground, like a swamp. Preston watches Stanley roll to a stop at his feet. With a glance at Tom, Preston smiles, tilts his head back, and screams like a rocket punching a hole in the darkening sky. He falls on top of Stanley. A few seconds later, the whole team, Tom included, is piled like dirty laundry in a puddle in front of the Wittsford goal.

Toppling off the pile and onto the wet grass, Tom catches Katya clapping her hands in the air, Mr. Gaz pounding his fists on the armrests of his wheelchair. Coach Palmisano jogs over and collects the ball. "Way to use the whole field, Tom," he says. "You pulled our defense all apart, there."

"Thanks," Tom says, still having difficulty connecting

his voice, what he has just witnessed, and reality.

Stanley jogs past him then as the teams resume their field positions. "Excellent pass," Stanley says. "We must've seen that empty space at just the same time."

"Right," Tom says. "That's how you beat these guys. Move to the space."

"Dude, we're, like, winning," Preston says, shaking his head as he draws alongside Tom and Stanley.

"Excellent deduction," Tom says, indulging himself a laugh as a tingling sensation dances along his limbs. "If you weren't homeschooled, I'd recommend you sign up for AP math."

"Pretty funny," Preston snickers, "for a jock."

After a bit of spot coaching from Palmisano, Wittsford tightens up its defense, playing conservatively while the Boosters keep up an enthusiastic offense—too enthusiastic, Tom realizes, noticing Jimmy bent over and gasping for air during one out-of-bounds whistle. The others look only slightly more energetic. As Tom has seen happen many times before, his teammates become sluggish in getting back on defense after offensive runs, despite his warnings and his own extra effort at filling in defensive gaps—gaps that become too numerous.

Wittsford scores, tying the game.

As the Boosters prepare to kick off again, Tom feels a hole forming in the pit of his stomach. Looking around the field at his team—smaller, weaker, muddier—he can predict the outcome without having to roll the ball another inch. Glancing at the sideline, he sees Katya and Mr. Gaz looking back at him, their arms folded in an identical way: critically.

Coach Palmisano gives a half toot on his whistle and nods to Tom, pointing to the ball resting on the center line. "Tom, we've got about two minutes to go before the half," he says, glancing at his watch.

Then lightning strikes—literally.

Coach Palmisano's eyes widen. "That's it," he says, stepping toward Tom, a hand extended. "We'll have to call this a tie. Good match, Tom."

As the man releases Tom's hand and commands his players to hit the locker room, Tom regards his teammates. Each one stands still, as if stuck in his own plot of quicksand. They look around—confused, stunned— then, one by one, turn to Tom.

"That's the match!" Tom shouts just as thunder breaks and another flash of lighting flickers around them.

"We tied?" Preston shouts through the rain.

Tom turns to him. "One!" he says, pointing at the Wittsford goal. "One," he repeats, pointing toward the Boosters' goal. "You do the math."

Preston howls into the sky again.

At another lightning flash, the Boosters sprint for the parking lot. Just as he's leaving the pitch, Tom spots Chaz Dempsey standing off by himself, hands drawn up into the sleeves of his Warriors varsity rain slicker.

Seeing Tom, Chaz jogs toward him.

Tom stops where he stands and stares at Chaz. Behind Chaz, Katya wheels Mr. Gaz quickly across the grass and onto the pavement.

"My dad said you had to tell me something," Chaz shouts over the downpour. "Tell me quick so I can get out of this crap."

Tom looks into the parking lot, where Katya has yanked open the van door and is loading her grandfather inside. Magnus and Jimmy, sealed safely inside the Volvo, are playing the timeless, childish game of locking the others out in the storm.

"Tell your father that you should be playing junior varsity," Tom says.

"Like hell."

"And tell him I'm going to prove it."

Tom can't make out what Chaz says next. The rain's coming down too hard, and he's running as fast as he can.

The thunder gets so loud, Tom thinks it might pop out the windows of the Good Egg as the Boosters settle in for a postgame meal. Tom mainly listens as his teammates replay the game, pass for pass, tackle for tackle. He laughs at the detail in which his teammates—especially the twins—remember, or *think* they remember, what was barely half a scrimmage.

Jimmy is silent. He stirs his milk shake—the only thing he ordered—while the others ramble on, packing food into their mouths between words. Occasionally Tom catches Jimmy staring out the window and into the night, his brow furrowing, his eyes taking on a steely look.

"I should've stopped that kid with the buzzcut," Stanley says, shaking his head while simultaneously cramming a half dozen french fries into his mouth.

"He was too fast," Magnus says. "He was going to score sooner or later."

Jimmy snorts under his breath, tosses some bills on the table, and stands up.

The others fall silent, their goofy smiles fading as Jimmy grabs his soaking wet sweatshirt from the adjacent booth. "I hope you're proud of yourselves," he says.

While Jimmy's head disappears inside the sweatshirt, Preston shoots Tom a confused look.

Tom shrugs. "So, you want to kick it around tomorrow, Jimmy?" he says.

Jimmy doesn't answer, staring into the darkness again.

"Weather's supposed to clear a little," Tom adds.

"Whatever," Jimmy mutters and starts for the door.

"Hold up," Preston says, grabbing Jimmy by the tail of his T-shirt.

Jimmy whirls around, looking ready to pound Preston into hamburger.

Preston gestures toward the back of the restaurant, where three guys in Southwind rain slickers are approaching—Paul Marcotte and two guys Tom doesn't recognize. One is a stocky kid with a stupid-looking goatee and a Boston Red Sox cap; the other is a scrawny, blue-haired kid with acne and an earring.

Jimmy meets them just short of the Boosters' booth. Preston leaps to his feet to stand next to him.

Tom looks at Magnus, who rolls his eyes and shakes his head. "Here we go."

"Table for three?" Preston sneers. "In the no-thinking section?"

"What's up, guys?" Paul says in what sounds to Tom like a genuinely cordial tone.

None of the Boosters responds.

"We just heard you guys tied Wittsford," the blue-haired kid says.

Paul flips his chin at Tom. "Is that true?"

Tom nods. "Yeah, sort of. We had to call it at the half . . . well, almost the half. But, yeah."

"What's it to you guys?" Preston says, taking a half step forward before Jimmy pulls him back.

"Well . . ." Paul stares Preston down. "We know you've got another big match coming up."

"The frick you talking about?" Jimmy mutters.

Paul locks eyes with Tom. "You mean, Tom hasn't told you?"

Preston, Jimmy, and the others turn to Tom.

"That's right," Tom says, picking up a fork and tapping it on the table.

Alex and Stanley simultaneously reach for the fork, so Tom sets it down.

"I kind of made a . . . I kind of set something up," Tom continues. "With Southwind."

"Southwind?" Preston says, twisting his face out of shape. "Haven't we boosted their morale enough?"

Jimmy snorts under his breath again. "Amazing," he says. "There's just never enough competition in life, is there?"

"I'd hardly call a grudge match with Southwind competition," Preston says. "It's more like an early Christmas present for them—"

"We played well today," Tom says, surprised at how stupid his own words sound—as if the Boosters wouldn't have been trounced if the Wittsford match hadn't been rained out.

No one says anything.

Tom reaches for the fork again but resists picking it up. "What else did Dempsey tell you?" he asks Paul.

"What do you mean?" Paul says.

Tom scans Paul's eyes, trying to determine if he's telling the whole truth, if he's telling everything he knows about the match with the Warriors.

"He says he wants them to go into the season with some confidence," Blue Hair says. "He says playing you guys ought to give them plenty."

Tom gives Paul a curious look. "You mean he wants *you* to go into the season with confidence."

Paul shakes his head. "No. *Them.* That's why we're here."

"To rub our noses in it?" Preston says. "You think you're so tough because of a stupid . . ."—he flicks Paul's left shoulder—"a stupid raincoat? Did Coach Dumpster give you a matching umbrella?" He moves to flick Paul's shoulder again, but Paul smacks his hand away. Preston lunges, but Jimmy holds him back.

"So, why are you here?" Jimmy says, looping his left arm around Preston's shoulders to restrain him.

"We want to play on your team," Paul says.

"You what?" Preston says.

Jimmy releases him.

"Yeah," Paul adds. "We're not going to get any playing time with Dempsey. Guy basically spelled it out for us. Exchange student from England took my spot."

"I can't stand Dempsey anyway," the kid in the Red Sox cap and goatee says.

Tom picks the fork up and points it at him, like a

knife-thrower in some teenage circus. "You're serious?"

"You don't know what Dempsey's like, Tom," Paul says.

Tom scans Paul's eyes again, then sets the fork down. "Oh, I can imagine," he says. He turns toward the street and catches the group's reflection in the darkened front window: nine forms against the black canvas. "Well, that's very interesting," he adds, letting his eye linger on Goatee's reflection. "The Boosters and I will have to talk this over. *These* Boosters, you know, not those other Boosters."

Goatee seems to be watching him, unaware that he himself is being watched in the reflection.

"I mean, with you three, that'd make nine. In a game of six on six, we'd have some subs."

"That'd be a lot less running," Jimmy says.

"Yeah." Tom turns back to the group, focusing on Goatee.

Goatee turns away, as if embarrassed about something.

"That could make a big difference," Tom says, still watching the kid.

Chapter 13

The Boosters, minus Preston, spread out near the picnic tables in Audette Park the next day, warming up for their final practice. Paul and his two Southwind defectors—Casey Blue Hair and Brad Goatee—knock the ball around in a circle with Magnus and Alex while Tom stretches and Stanley juggles nearby. Tom watches Jimmy sitting on a picnic table and smoking a cigarette. Jimmy glances around occasionally—nervously, it seems to Tom. Tom recalls the first day he spotted Jimmy hanging out in the park and those other guys in the SUV, how Jimmy hadn't wanted to play soccer unless they could do it somewhere else. And so began this whole mess.

And how many chances did I have to get out of it? Tom asks himself, sitting up and leaning forward to touch the tips of his cleats—his old screw-ins. The grass is still a little wet, and the cleats he wore yesterday are fossilized in dried mud. *You are one slow learner, Gray,* he says. A second later, he spots Preston clambering up out of the swing set pit, dribbling a ball somewhat listlessly.

As Preston draws a few steps closer, Tom can see the bruises on his face, a stitched-up gash over his left eye.

"Morning, freaks," Preston says, throwing his backpack down. "Pardon my appearance. I took a little spill coming out of the library this morning."

"Who did it?" Jimmy asks without a trace of emotion,

as if asking Preston where he bought his backpack.

"Some Southwind players—oh, sorry, I mean *Warriors*. Yes, that fighting spirit at the heart of the Warrior—ah!" He clenches his side. "At the heart of the Warrior tradition. I was ambushed by three of them, I think. My math gets a little fuzzy after a few blows to the head."

"What'd you do?" Magnus says in a flat tone.

"*I* didn't do anything," Preston says. "I was coming out of the library, and these guys jumped—"

"No, what did you do to *them?*" Magnus cuts him off.

Tom shoots Magnus a confused look. "What did *Preston* do to *them?*"

Preston laughs, even though it obviously causes him pain. "Ah, Magnus," he says, sitting down and pulling his cleats out of his pack. "You know me too well."

"What are you guys talking about?" Tom says.

Preston takes a cell phone from his backpack and holds it up to Tom. "The numbers," he cackles. "They don't lie."

"What are you going to do, call someone in for payback?" Jimmy says, pacing. "You don't need to call someone, dude. I'm standing right here. Three, four, five of them—I don't care. Who were they—"

"Math is a language!" Preston shouts into the sky.

"You're sick," Magnus says.

Tom looks at Magnus, then at Preston. "What's going on?"

Preston cackles again and tosses his cell phone back into his pack. "Nothing's going on, Tom," he says.

Tom suddenly remembers the day he and Preston first met, the way Preston had used his cell phone to launch his rocket, then unsuccessfully tried to use it to activate the landing mechanism. "Is that cell phone wired to something?" he says.

Magnus storms off.

Tom turns to Alex and Stanley, who are watching Preston with fear in their eyes.

"No," Preston says. "It's not wired to anything. Yet."

Magnus whirls around from where he sulks, twenty yards or so away. "Ask him about getting kicked out of Southwind!"

Tom turns to Preston, who's lacing up his cleats, smiling to himself. "I used to go to Southwind, it's true," he says. "I was asked to leave. Hence my participation in some mandatory, extracurricular anger management programs."

"Why did you get booted?" Tom says. "Did you blow something up?"

Preston stands, pulls up his socks, and begins stretching. "I've said it before, Tom. You can't let people push you around." He turns to Jimmy. "Isn't that right, Jimmy? Bullies need to be taught a lesson—ow!" Preston grabs his left side. "Bruised a rib here. Now, these bullies may need more than one lesson before they get it—"

"This is insane," Jimmy grumbles, booting a ball aimlessly into the park.

Tom watches the ball come to a roll just shy of the swing set—a pretty nice blast. When he turns back, Jimmy is stuffing his cleats inside a plastic shopping bag. "Where you going?" Tom says.

Jimmy doesn't answer.

"Maybe he's got some homework to do," Preston says,

still stretching. "You know how it is with us homeschoolers. Work, work, work."

Jimmy takes three strides toward Preston and looms over him. "You know what?" he mutters. "I'm not surprised you got your ass kicked, with that smart mouth of yours." He flips the plastic bag over his shoulder, and Preston reels back to avoid getting hit in the face with it. Jimmy spits and walks away.

"Jimmy," Tom calls, "we've got a game tomorrow. Southwind field, one o'clock."

Jimmy keeps walking.

"Are you going to be there, Jimmy?"

Jimmy backpedals. "I don't know, Tom," he shouts. "I've got a *ton* of homework. You know, 'work, work, work.'" He turns around just as a copper-colored SUV pulls in.

Tom watches as the SUV pulls up to the curb and Jimmy approaches the passenger window. The tinted glass rolls down and a hand reaches out. Jimmy shakes it and gives it an obviously familiar series of palm slaps and knuckle raps, exchanging words with someone sitting inside. A couple seconds later, the back door opens and Jimmy hops in.

"He's not really homeschooled, is he?" Tom says, watching the SUV pull out of the lot.

"You're catching on," Preston says, executing a nice rainbow, even with his hands pressed to his chest as if to keep his ribs from falling out. "Yeah, you're learning real fast."

Chapter 14

Mr. Gaz is even more animated than usual during the chalk-talk at the store that night. Tom doesn't pay much attention, preoccupied by Jimmy's absence. *What's his problem?* he wonders. *It's not like anyone forced him to play on our team.*

He mentally sets up the field, factoring in a potential Jimmy no-show: Marcotte at stopper, Casey Blue Hair at a wing fullback, and Brad Goatee at sweeper . . .

He feels a little guilty about tuning out Mr. Gaz, but he gets the gist of the old man's lecture soon after Katya begins translating. He's mainly identifying those things that the Boosters did well against Wittsford: running to support the player with the ball, providing an outlet pass; playing the ball to open spaces; switching the field often with long, crossing passes that pull the defense apart as they shift to meet the advance from a new direction. On this last point, Mr. Gaz falters for a moment, firing off a rapid exchange with Katya.

"*Da! Da!*" she says, turning to Tom. "He's looking for a word to describe this . . . this candy that you pull."

"Taffy," Preston says before Tom can answer.

"Yes," Katya says, flashing Preston a smile. "I can always count on my English teacher."

Tom feels a little jealous dagger.

Mr. Gaz grumbles something, and Katya turns away.

Preston winks at Tom, stitches dancing above his eye.

After the chalk-talk, Tom decides to linger, hoping to catch Katya alone. For a moment, it looks as if he might get away with it, but as his teammates make their way down the store's center aisle, Preston turns and notices him still leaning against the front counter. Katya's in the office, out of view, and from where Tom stands, it sounds as though she's arguing with someone. He thinks he knows who it is. Though he has never heard the Hood speak, the low voice responding to Katya's rant doesn't sound like Mr. Gaz.

Preston says something to Magnus, and the others all turn and follow Preston back up the aisle toward the counter.

"You don't want a ride home?" Magnus says, spinning his car keys on his finger.

"No, thanks," Tom says. "I'm not ready to go yet."

"Just remember," Preston says. "We have a game tomorrow. No making out with Russian spies before the match."

"That sounds like something Jimmy might say," Tom says.

Preston's smirk fades. "Speaking of whom . . ."

Tom sighs. "I hope he shows. He's a part of the team, part of the flow."

"And I think he's down to a pack a day," Preston adds.

Tom sighs again, shaking his head.

"Well," Preston says, "we certainly don't want to interrupt your after-hours . . . shopping, Tom. So, the boys and I will just say good night."

"See you tomorrow," Tom says.

Preston and the others continue down the aisle and out the door.

Katya blusters through the curtain separating the office and the shop, her face red with exertion or rage. She seems both startled and annoyed to find Tom standing at the counter as if waiting to have a purchase rung up. "What are you doing here?" she says.

"Uh, I wanted to talk to you." He stares at his Sambas.

"Why? The shop is closed."

"I know, but . . . I don't know." Tom gazes down the center aisle. "I feel like over these past weeks . . ." He turns back to Katya and finds her zoning out on the floor behind the register, her jaw set, her blue eyes seeming to burn a hole in something below the counter. "I'm sorry," Tom adds and starts for the door. "I just really like you." His face lights up like a campfire as he heads quickly down the aisle.

"Tom!" Katya calls after him.

His heart racing, he stops and faces her again. As soon as their eyes meet, however, he hears the jingle of the bells over the front door. Katya's eyes focus beyond him.

"The shop is closed," she says firmly.

Tom turns to the door just as Coach Dempsey slips in.

"Oh, I don't want to buy anything," Dempsey says, fixing Tom with a grin. "I'm just here to talk to this guy. How you doing, Tom?" Dempsey extends his hand.

Although Tom doesn't want to shake it, he remembers his father's words—"*When a man, even your worst enemy, extends his hand, you are the lesser if you don't take it*"—and grips Dempsey's damp hand for just long enough to count as a handshake. "Hey, Coach," Tom says, reflexively wiping his hand on his pants.

Dempsey leans one shoulder against the wall of boxes and crosses his arms, his head about even with a row of ant farm kits. Tom notices the little white crow's feet cutting through Dempsey's pink, hamlike skin around his eyes and in puppet lines extending down from the sides of his mouth. *The man has been getting some sun,* he thinks, and speculates that his players, as usual, have been getting plenty of exercise.

"I just came to wish you luck tomorrow," Dempsey adds.

"Thanks," Tom says. "Same to you."

The coach smiles. "You sound like you think there's going to be any contest whatsoever."

"There might be. We play pretty hard now."

Dempsey shakes his head, shifts his weight to his other shoulder. "Yes, I understand you tied Wittsford for a half."

Tom feels the blood returning to his face. He glances toward the counter, but Katya is gone.

"Tom," Dempsey says in a somber tone, "enough is enough. You're mixed up in this whole mascot debate when you don't need to be—"

"I'll decide what I need and don't need."

Dempsey takes a deep breath and stares at the shop door. "What I mean," he continues, turning back to Tom, "is that I think you're carrying this whole ridiculous mascot debate on your shoulders, when you really are free to do what you want to do, which is play competitive soccer, maybe even get yourself a college scholarship. Am I right?"

Tom looks up at the ceiling. "No," he says, trying to stay calm but feeling his heart starting to pound. "I mean, yes and no."

Dempsey snorts under his breath. "How's that?"

Tom looks at him. "Yes, I'm free to do what I want to do. But, no, it's not just play soccer. And, no, the mascot debate isn't ridiculous."

Dempsey shakes his head. "You lost me."

"I've got to honor what I believe in."

"Well, I can certainly respect that. But, you see, that's just what people aren't getting about the Warrior mascot. They don't understand that when we honor our tradition, we honor the people who came before—"

"By using the symbol of an Indian? What about the Native Americans who prefer to be treated like people, not a mascot—"

"But we honor *that* tradition too—your tradition, Tom. A tribute to the bravery of those people. Your people—"

"People you offer nothing else, just . . . a 'tribute,' as you call it. Some people think that a better tribute might be to help—"

"See, that's just the point. Some people have made this whole thing political, and when you do that, it pulls people apart. I won't stand for it. I can't stand for it. I owe it . . ." Dempsey hesitates, turning away, staring into the gray shade of dusk lowering over the shop window.

Tom takes a deep breath, remembering that black-and-white team photograph in the Southwind trophy case: the 1967 Warrior football squad. "You owe it to your old football team," he says. "Especially the guys who went off to Vietnam."

Dempsey snaps his head around.

Tom is tempted to step back, but he holds his ground.

"You haven't got the right to speak about them—"

"Why not?" Tom counters, struggling to keep his voice from cracking. "I know some Vietnam vets up at Kawehras. In fact, my uncle Bo fought in Vietnam."

Dempsey gives Tom a look that seems to teeter between anger and sadness. "Then your uncle Bo would remember the way that politics robbed those men—warriors, every last one of them—of the honor they deserved. They were heroes, but people treated them as villains."

"You volunteered to fight in Vietnam."

Dempsey pauses and stares out the window again. "I owed it to them—then as now. I honored them."

Tom takes another deep breath and gazes back up the empty aisle. "Then we have a problem," he says. "Because I also have to honor someone who's no longer here." As he utters the words, he lets his eyes wander up the toy-box walls, rising like skyscrapers flanking this narrow, empty boulevard. It occurs to him that he has never seen the cities that his father and the other Kawehras ironworkers built. He wonders if he ever will.

For what seems like a long time, the two of them say nothing. The only sound in the shop is the flickering of the old ceiling lights.

"We have two right answers," Dempsey finally says with what sounds to Tom like a slightly bitter laugh.

Tom turns to find the coach still staring out the window, hands clasped behind his back as he rocks on his sneakers. "Seems that way," Tom says.

Dempsey shrugs. "And, so, we fight."

"We don't have to."

"I'm afraid we do."

"But we've got options. I heard that someone suggested a shield, or maybe a knight in armor, instead of the Indian."

Dempsey shakes his head and looks at the boxes in front of him, his gaze seeming to grow distant. "You've never seen a more tight-knit team in your life, Tom," he says. "Like brothers, we were."

Unsure of how to respond, Tom is silent. The old lamps buzzing overhead again fill the shop with an uncomfortable energy. "Change it," he says to fill the awkward lull. "Change the mascot."

"I can't." Dempsey crosses his arms. "All I can do is offer you a deal. My final offer." He leans back on the ant farm shelf. "Forget this match tomorrow."

"What?"

"Just forget it. We cancel it. *I* cancel it, if you like."

"And then what?"

"You come and play for the Warriors—"

"I can't do—"

"Hear me out." Dempsey gestures with his hands as if holding an invisible loaf of bread. "Play one game . . ." He chops in the air with his right hand. "Play two games . . ." He waggles his left hand. "Hell, I don't care." He drops his hands to his sides. "Just join the team and play. Give it a try. Quit if it still bugs you that much."

"So, what's in it for me?" Tom says.

"What's in it for you is that if you play at least one game for me, you won't be obligated to play for the Warriors for the next two seasons, which . . ."—he points toward the street—"is what you'll owe me come this time tomorrow night."

Tom feels his stomach churning as he considers Dempsey's proposal. *One game*, he thinks. *I could suit up for one lousy game with those guys, then quit, and this whole thing would be over and done with.*

As Dempsey shifts his weight and puts his hands on his hips, Tom focuses on the man's hands—pinkish brown hands the color of a newborn hamster, with swirls of wiry hair drawing clouds on the backs.

"You were in the zone, Tom. Yes, I think you were . . . Anyone walking along a narrow beam so high up in the air is right to be afraid . . . We depend on each other. And we get so we can communicate without even speaking sometimes."

The words echo in Tom's thoughts as he turns his attention back to the register. Again, no Katya.

Turning back to Dempsey, he sees the beads of sweat working their way down the man's temples. "No," Tom says.

Dempsey nods, as if expecting this response, and pushes off the ant farms again to stand in the center of the aisle. He tucks his golf shirt into his shorts with a quickness that suggests to Tom that he's channeling anger somewhere. "Well, if that's your decision, then that's your decision," he says in a clipped, formal tone. He extends a hand.

Tom shakes Dempsey's hand, but the man holds on.

"There's just one other thing," Dempsey says. "You

128

realize that we're going full field tomorrow."

"What?" Tom pulls on his hand, but Dempsey holds on.

"Yeah. See, when you and I spoke a couple weeks ago, we agreed that *your team* and *my team* would play one more match before the regular season starts. Well . . ."— Dempsey finally releases Tom's hand and stands back, nodding toward the street again—"my team has eleven players. Check your rule book, and I think you'll find that soccer the world over is played with eleven players."

"You never said that—"

"I said we'd play a soccer match, Tom. Now, what does that mean to you? Should I get a dictionary?" Dempsey narrows his eyes. "Last chance. We can call the whole thing off."

Tom just glares back.

"One o'clock, Tom," Dempsey says, turning for the door. "I suggest you get a good night's rest."

Tom stares at the floor, holding his breath until the bells above the front door are silent. He smacks the wall of boxes behind him and groans.

Katya comes around the corner suddenly, a feather duster in one hand, a bottle of neon blue cleanser in the other. "Don't damage the merchandise," she says, moving directly to straighten the ant farm boxes across from Tom.

"Sorry," Tom says.

Katya turns to him, standing more or less where Dempsey had been standing a few moments earlier. "You made a deal with that man," she says, waving her duster in the air.

"Yes," Tom says. "Were you listening?"

"It's my store." She crosses the aisle and, shooing Tom

to one side, straightens the boxes behind him. "But, tell me. You made a bet with him?"

Tom nods.

"If your team plays his team tomorrow, and you lose . . ."

"I have to play on his team for the next two years."

"The *Eeen*-dians team?"

"Right."

"*Da,*" Katya says, squirting the cleanser toward the ceiling. She turns to Tom and rests her hands on her hips, the spray bottle and feather duster like pistols at her sides. "But he said that you'll play full field. Eleven players."

"Right."

Katya passes him on her way back to the front counter, where she sets her cleaning gear on the counter and hoists herself up so that she's facing Tom. "But you only have nine players," she calls down to him. "Is that correct?"

Tom advances a few steps in her direction. "That's right. I basically blew the whole deal."

Katya says nothing until Tom has reached the counter. She spins back behind the counter and disappears into the darkened office. A second later, she kills the shop lights.

Alone in the dark, silent store, he strains his eyes to follow Katya's movement back in the office, not knowing whether to follow her over the counter or leave the shop. Forever.

A desk lamp flicks on in the office, illuminating Katya pulling a book from a drawer. She sets it on the desk and turns toward Tom, beckoning with a finger.

Tom clears the front counter as if it were a hurdle.

Katya pulls out the desk chair and directs him to sit.

"Here," she says, opening the book—a sturdy album of some sort giving off a musty odor. "This is my grandfather's."

"Mr. Gaz's."

"*Da.* Yes."

The first few pages of the album contain black-and-white photographs of soccer players. Each photograph has a caption written in someone's elegant hand—but in an alphabet Tom doesn't understand.

Flipping a few pages ahead, Katya presses a finger on the forehead of a young man standing in the center of the back row of a team photo.

Tom reads the caption. Among the strange lettering he sees the word *Dynamo* in English characters.

"This is him," Katya says, pulling her finger away. "The Moscow Dynamo."

She pronounces it *"Dee-na-mo."*

Tom looks up, noticing the Hood emerging from the darkened shop. He and the Hood lock eyes for a moment before the Hood reaches into the office and flicks a switch. Tom and Katya are suddenly bathed in sterile, fluorescent light.

"They were the top Soviet team," the Hood says, stepping into the office. "One of the best teams in the world, actually."

Tom notes the similarly precise enunciation of the c's, t's, and l's in the Hood's accent as in Katya's—*"eh-ctually."*

Katya says something to her brother in Russian that

Tom can't understand, but he gathers that she's less than overjoyed to have an older-brother chaperon at this particular moment.

The Hood listens patiently, then crosses the room to stand on the other side of the desk. "I'm Yuri," he says, extending a hand and pushing the hood off, exposing a fairly normal-looking guy with straight black hair, not the best skin in the world, and Katya's death-ray blue eyes. "I'm her brother."

Tom shakes Yuri's hand. "I'm Tom."

"And you're in some kind of trouble, I know. I heard you talking to that guy, that . . . unpleasant military man."

"Why were you listening?" Tom says, repeating to himself Yuri's pronunciation of *"mee-lee-tary."*

"You like my sister," Yuri says, "and I'm a protective brother."

Katya groans and disappears into the house.

"She seems to take care of herself pretty well," Tom says.

Yuri shakes his head and sits on the edge of the desk across from Tom. "Our parents . . .," he begins to say.

"I know. Same thing for my father. A car crash."

Yuri gestures around the office. "And now this," he says. "Welcome to our toy shop. Our science toy shop. It's a busy place. We are always working."

Katya returns and exchanges a few sharp words with her brother in Russian, initiating, as Yuri stands, a debate that moves around the office.

In hopes of staying out of the discussion, Tom flips through the album, checking out mostly black-and-white photos of Mr. Gazzayev and his teammates. After a few of these pictures, he digs his finger way into the back pages of the album and flips the pages over. There, in brilliant color, he discovers a picture of two children, a boy and a girl about six or seven years old, dressed in soccer uniforms and hugging a man Tom identifies as Mr. Gaz minus about ten years.

Yuri's finger suddenly reaches over Tom's arm and presses the page.

Tom follows the sweatshirt arm up to Yuri's face.

"He is a Soviet legend," Yuri says. "Listen closely to what he says. Every word is . . . soccer poetry."

"He taught us everything," Katya says, returning to sit on the desk just inches from Tom's hand.

"Yes, but with our store now," Yuri says in a tone that seems to be correcting a mistake, "we have little time for such things."

"Leetle time for satch theengs . . ."

This begins another debate between Katya and Yuri, during which Tom keeps flipping through the album.

"And you need two players," Katya says, her sudden shift back to English catching him off-guard.

Tom turns to Yuri. "You're soccer players?"

Without answering, Yuri flips the album ahead a few more pages to a spread of yellowed newspaper clippings, the words dancing across the page in those indecipherable characters.

Yuri and Katya continue their debate in Russian, and Tom examines the newspaper photos, since he can't read the words. They all feature either Yuri or Katya in action. He flips to the next page and finds more. He flips ahead to the last pages in the album and finds still more news clippings of Yuri and Katya, including one—the last item in the album—with a photo of Yuri and Katya together, each with an arm around the other and a trophy in hand. They seem to Tom only a couple years younger than they are today.

"So," Yuri finally says, smiling wryly at Tom, Katya, and Tom again. "We can play. One match. It's decided."

Tom looks at Katya, who smiles that gap-toothed smile. "Why didn't you tell me you play soccer?" he says.

"You never asked."

He turns to Yuri. "I thought you were a freak."

"I *am* a freak," Yuri says, walking back out into the store. "But I was watching out for my little sister."

Katya groans again, then rests a hand on Tom's forearm.

Tom rolls his arm and pulls his hand forward, catching Katya's strong fingers in his own. Turning toward the store, he sees Yuri step out of view. A second later, he feels Katya's other hand on his face.

"But now I'm sure that she's safe," Yuri shouts from somewhere inside the store. "Pretty sure, anyway."

"She is," Tom manages to say, but just barely.

Chapter 15

Tom is wigged out, as Katya pulls the Nucleus van into the Southwind High School parking lot, to find a crowd of nearly a hundred people scattered throughout the bleachers. He hadn't counted on this. *Must be Dempsey got the word out,* he thinks.

As he steps into the muggy, slate gray afternoon, wisps of dirty-cotton clouds drifting overhead, he spots Pamela Routly and a photographer chatting with Preston off to the side of the Boosters' bench. A referee in full uniform alternately stretches and checks his watch a few yards away from them. Approaching the field, Tom sees a group of about a dozen people sitting with a SOUTHWIND ATHLETIC BOOSTERS banner across their laps. The boosters don't boo Tom as he walks to his team's bench, but they get quiet in a way that makes him nervous.

He sees his mother in the bleachers, sitting alone. Catching his eye, she waves.

Katya says something to Yuri in Russian.

He responds in a low voice.

"This brings back memories for us," Katya says.

"For me too," Tom says, glancing at his mother again. She's still watching him, as if the game has already begun and he's carrying the ball down the field. He can almost see his father sitting next to her.

Tom helps Yuri lift Mr. Gaz out of the van, and Katya

begins pushing his wheelchair toward the field. Walking a few steps ahead and watching Preston and the others stretching and warming up, Tom notices something wrong. He counts his teammates' heads just to be sure: Jimmy is missing.

Dropping back alongside Mr. Gaz's wheelchair, Tom sneaks a peek at the old man's watch: 12:40. "Damn," he mutters to himself.

"What's the problem?" Katya says.

"Jimmy."

"The smoking guy," Yuri says.

"Right."

"He should play in goal," Yuri adds. "He has good hands. No fear, but very weak lungs."

"Problem is," Tom says, "he's not here."

As Tom tosses his backpack onto the ground, Preston jogs over from his interview. He cracks a smile, noticing two new players tossing their gear into the Boosters' camp. "I had a feeling you were holding out on us, Katya," he says. "Like a sneaky Russian spy."

"You watch too many videos," she says, pushing Mr. Gaz's wheelchair toward the sideline.

"I'm her brother," Yuri says, extending a hand to Preston. "Also a spy. I'm your center midfielder."

"Welcome to the team," Preston says, shaking Yuri's hand. Preston turns toward the other Boosters, who are spread out in front of the goal, passing the ball to one another, juggling, stretching. "That means we have even more subs now, right?"

"Not exactly," Tom says. "We're playing full sides — and full field."

Preston is silent for a few seconds. "Come again?"

Tom almost blurts out his bet with Dempsey, but he holds back. "Yeah," he says. "Since it's our last game, Dempsey and I decided to take it to the next level."

"Did he, by any chance, offer to lend you a player or two? Because by my count, we're down a man."

"I realize that." Tom scans the perimeter of the athletic field, as if expecting Jimmy to leap like a deer from the trees. "We have to find him. Do you know where he's staying?"

"I doubt he's *staying* anywhere," Preston mutters. "Homeschooled, my butt—"

"The park," Tom says. "Maybe he's there."

Katya returns and begins digging gear out of her bag. She's wearing sky blue shorts, lime green soccer socks, and a lime green jersey with fading Russian characters in white.

"Katya," Tom says. "We need to drive to the park—quickly."

Looking up, Katya shakes her head and groans that special, exasperated groan that Tom knows women reserve for the stupid mistakes of men. "Quickly," she says, plunging her hand inside her gear bag and retrieving the van keys.

"Kveekly," Tom repeats to himself as they begin jogging toward the van.

Pulling into the Audette Park lot, Tom spots Jimmy sitting on a picnic table, smoking and looking onto the empty field. He turns toward the van, blows smoke, then turns back to the park. It seems to Tom as if Jimmy has been waiting for him, except that he's not dressed for soccer. He's wearing his cargo pants, black boots, and a stretched-out gray T-shirt.

Tom and Katya get out of the van and jog over to him.

Jimmy drags on his cigarette and leans back, elbows resting on the picnic table.

"Jimmy," Tom says as he and Katya reach him, "what's the deal?"

Jimmy says nothing.

Tom walks around to face him. "Kickoff's in, like, fifteen minutes, dude—"

"Then you better hurry back," Jimmy says, staring past Tom and flicking his cigarette right at him, as if he's not even there.

Tom jumps out of the way. "What's the problem, Jimmy? We've got one more game. Just one more."

Jimmy snorts and looks at Tom. "Just one more," he repeats. "Do you really believe that?"

"What do you mean?"

"I mean, do you really think this is the last game?"

"Well, probably. I mean, for our team anyway. The regular season is starting next week—"

"I'm not talking about any *season*. I'm just talking about games."

"Games—"

"Right. These games that everyone gets so amped up about. Games to see who's better. Games to prove whose school is better, whose kid is better—"

"But this isn't about any of that, Jimmy. That's the whole point. We aren't on the school team—"

"No, but now it's become just like that." Jimmy gets up and walks to the edge of the picnic area, where he pulls a pack of cigarettes from his pocket and jogs another one out.

"I don't get it," Tom says. "I thought you liked playing with us. I mean, no one made you do it."

"That's right," Jimmy says flatly. "And no one's going to make me play today either."

Tom looks at Katya, whose eyes are shooting sapphire lasers at Jimmy. "You could've told me," Tom says.

With the toe of his boot, Jimmy digs a piece of broken glass out of the dirt, bends over, and picks it up. "What difference would it've made?" he says, tossing the glass into the nearest trash barrel, ten feet away.

"Dude, we're playing the Warriors full field."

At this, Jimmy turns to Tom, but he shrugs his shoulders a couple of seconds later and looks away. "I guess you're going to get some exercise, then." He lights his cigarette. "Anyway, you picked up some new players the other night."

"Are you bugging that we have Southwind guys on the team?"

Jimmy shakes his head and takes a drag. "Makes no fricking difference to me, guy. It just seems like, with that newspaper article and everything, this is turning into just another game—like you said. Just another game where a bunch of kids run around so a bunch of parents can feel superior to another bunch of parents." He gives Tom a chin flip. "I bet there's quite a crowd over there at Southwind, isn't there?"

Tom nods. "But it's not about the crowd," he says. "And it's not about being superior."

"Then what is it about?"

Tom takes a deep breath and gazes out over the field. "For me, it's . . . personal."

Jimmy takes a drag and pauses for a moment. "Personal in what way?"

Tom takes another deep breath and looks at Katya, trying to decide whether he should tell Jimmy why he and Dempsey are colliding again. "Put it this way," he says. "My father would want me to beat Dempsey—or at least try my hardest."

Jimmy holds his cigarette up, staring at the smoke trickling from the glowing tip. "My father would want to beat Dempsey himself," he says. "Then he'd want to beat me—so he would."

"Is that why you ran away from home?"

Jimmy pauses in mid-drag, his eyes widening, then narrowing, as if he's both surprised and angry that Tom has discovered his secret. He finishes his drag and flips his chin at Tom again. "Who told you that?"

"Preston."

"How did he find out?"

"I don't know, but he knows. We all know, actually. We've sort of known for a while."

At this, Jimmy looks away, as though toward the soccer field where Preston and the others are waiting. "You all knew," he says, "but you didn't say anything?"

"What were we supposed to say? That you couldn't play without a note from your parents?"

Jimmy makes that snort under his breath again. "That would've been difficult."

"For me, impossible," Katya says.

Jimmy turns to her, finally seeming to notice that her

jersey, shorts, and socks all match. He turns to Tom. "Is she playing?"

Tom nods. "Her brother too."

"The freak in the sweatshirt?" Jimmy says.

"Yeah, and he's supposedly a star. But let's be honest," Tom adds, "is there a kid on our team who *isn't* a freak?"

Jimmy snorts out a quick laugh but almost immediately stares at the ground with a scowl. "I don't have any gear," he mutters.

"What happened to it?"

Jimmy drops his cigarette and grinds it out with his boot. "Left it somewhere."

"Your friends find it?"

Jimmy pauses, his expression darkening. "They're not my friends."

"Then why do you hang with them?"

Jimmy looks toward the parking lot, his eyes taking on a faraway look. "You wouldn't understand." He sighs. "Running away's a lot more complicated than I thought it would be. You think you're getting away from certain kinds of people, but, then, there they are again."

"Well, gear's not a huge problem," Tom says, trying to sound upbeat. "You're playing net anyway."

Jimmy cracks a faint smile. "I haven't played net since I was a kid."

"Let's just hope you remember something," Tom says.

"I bet I remember a lot." Jimmy chuckles. "I remember there wasn't much running involved."

"We should run now," Katya says, jingling the van keys. "And quickly."

"*Kveekly.*"

141

Tom can see the Boosters and the Warriors standing in their field positions as Katya wheels into the Southwind lot. The instant she touches the breaks, Jimmy whips open the side door, letting in the unmistakable trill of a referee's whistle. He and Tom fly out of the van and sprint toward the field, Katya trailing a few steps behind.

At the field, Jimmy runs immediately into the goalie box, his eyes fixed on the action developing along the left side of the field. Stopping, he begins rolling up his pant legs.

Preston gets the ball at the left-wing midfield and, immediately surrounded by Southwind players, dishes a panicked pass back to Magnus.

"Kick it out!" Tom shouts as he and Katya reach the pitch.

Magnus boots the ball over the sideline, across the running track, and onto the adjacent field hockey field.

By the time the Warriors pick it up, throw it in, and begin their downfield advance, Tom and Katya are running onto the field and into position. "Replace Alex on the wing," Tom shouts to her. "Alex! Drop back—"

"No! I'll play in the center," Katya answers, following with a string of Russian words for Yuri.

Center? Tom says to himself, nearly stopping in his tracks. *But I'm the center striker.*

"Tom, play in front of me," Yuri calls to him, back-pedaling quickly as Southwind strings together passes across the middle of the field. "I'm your defensive center midfielder. You play offensive center midfield."

"Who's my man?" Tom shouts, but Yuri dashes across the field, intercepting a pass between two Warriors.

He dribbles the ball ahead a few yards, then, just as two Warriors converge on him, heels the ball to Tom without so much as a glance back.

Tom traps the ball and looks downfield.

"Look for Katya!" Yuri commands.

The second he says this, Tom catches, out of the corner of his eye, Katya's blond head breaking from the center of the field to the right side. Turning, he spots a wide-open parcel of turf twenty yards ahead of her.

"Man on!" Preston shouts from Tom's left.

Tom pulls the ball toward himself with the bottom of his right foot, shields it with the left side of his body, and drags the ball around, clockwise, in a complete circle.

The Southwind player, following the ball, gets caught in Tom's revolving door and ends up behind Tom's back when Tom is facing downfield again.

The move gives Tom just enough time to push the ball forward a yard and drive it into the vacant patch of grass ahead of Katya.

Arriving at the plot simultaneously with the ball, Katya executes a flawless trap, settles the ball, dribbles a few yards, and crosses it to the opposite side of the field.

"Stay wide!" Preston shouts a split second before Tom was about to yell the exact same thing.

Alex, on his run down the left side of the field, has drifted in toward the center, and Katya's pass flies over his head.

A whistle. Out of bounds.

As the Warriors move around, getting open for their throw-in, Tom looks for an unmarked player. "Who's my man in this formation?" he calls to Yuri, who's jogging toward the Southwind center midfielder, Greg Plutakis, a stocky but fast kid with a dark shadow of beard.

"You don't play defense!" Yuri answers. "Carry the ball or pass to the strikers!"

"What?"

"Special European formation," Yuri shouts before the ball sails into play, landing at Greg Plutakis's feet. Yuri is immediately on him, forcing Plutakis to dish off to the stopper back, who, pressured by Katya, dishes back to the sweeper, Kyle Erdmann. With a three-step running start, Kyle kicks the ball on a roll, sending it way downfield, over the center circle and into the Boosters' end. Magnus makes a chest trap and settles the ball, turning it back to Brad Goatee at sweeper.

Goatee carries the ball out to the right sideline, where, despite being all alone, he trips, stumbles, and regains his footing—but only after letting the ball trickle out of bounds. The crowd reacts with disappointment, except for the Southwind Boosters.

Tom looks up at the row of them. A few shake their heads at him.

As the Warrior strikers and midfielders begin flooding the Boosters' defensive end for the throw-in, Tom watches his teammates dropping back, picking up unmarked players. Spotting a Warrior middie beginning a run deeper into the Boosters' end, Tom starts to call Preston to drop back farther.

Before he can get a word out, though, Preston turns, sprints ten yards ahead of the player, then begins a side-shuffling jog to contain him.

Good, conservative defense, Tom thinks.

"Alex, slide over!" Preston shouts.

Tom watches Alex pick up the player Preston had been marking a few moments before.

Then, with a few quick directions from Yuri, the entire Boosters team shifts to match up with the Warriors' offensive push. Tom eyes Kyle and the right-wing fullback, who both hang way back, out of danger. They're the only unmarked Warriors, and Tom is the only Booster without someone to contain, meaning, he realizes, that with the Boosters' one-player advantage on defense, he can wander into open space to receive a pass if his team gets the ball. It seems to him that the Boosters received some coaching while he and Katya were getting Jimmy, and Yuri's strategy is beginning to make sense.

The throw-in reaches a Warrior midfielder, who knocks the ball to the center midfielder—Yuri's man. Yuri shadows the kid to the right of the field, forcing him to dish off to the right-wing fullback, who sprints up from the Warrior defense.

Tom spots Preston's mark starting to slip in behind him again as Preston hesitates between stepping up to the fullback carrying the ball and sticking with the midfielder. "Behind you, Preston!" he shouts as Katya approaches the fullback with the ball. She's a step too late, though, and the fullback sends a long pass over Preston's head and into the right corner of the field, where it's picked up by the Warrior middie Preston allowed to drift past him. "He's offsides!" Tom shouts, noticing that the Warrior player had been standing a good five yards deeper into the

Boosters end than the deepest Booster player before the fullback sent him the ball—blatantly offsides. He glares at the ref.

Jogging past, the man eyes him sternly and taps at the yellow and red penalty cards poking out of his shirt pocket.

Tom turns back to the action just as the Warrior midfielder sends a long pass in front of the Boosters' goal.

"Mine!" Jimmy shouts, shoving his way out of the goal mouth—literally smacking one kid in the head—and punching the ball out of the air and toward the right sideline. Two Warriors hit the ground in the process, each grabbing some body part in an Academy Award–worthy display of agony.

The ref blows the whistle and jogs toward Jimmy, clenching the whistle in his teeth like a dog carrying a chew toy.

Tom walks toward them to see what the problem is and notices something strange: Goatee standing way out on the right wing, almost to the sideline—nowhere near where he should've been when the Warrior midfielder sent the ball across the goal mouth. Tom doesn't know Goatee's game at all, having never played against him as a Raven, but he can't imagine what thought process would lead a sweeperback way out to the wing on a cross-field pass. He catches Goatee's eye as he approaches Jimmy, Yuri, and the ref, but Goatee looks down and jogs back toward the center—a more normal field position.

"I'll give you two choices," the ref barks at Jimmy, sounding, to Tom, a lot more serious than scrimmage refs usually sound. "You find another pair of shoes or you don't play. Understand?"

Jimmy squints at the man for a couple of seconds without saying anything.

"And," the ref adds, "I can give you a yellow card for just looking at me that way."

Tom sees Magnus rifling through the team's gear at their bench. The Swede yanks a pair of dorky-looking Swedish sneakers out of his pack and sprints back onto the field. "Here," he says from a few yards away.

"Better than fricking nothing," Jimmy grumbles. He storms over to the goalpost and begins unlacing his boots.

"You watch your mouth, keeper," the ref hisses, gesturing for a Warrior player to flip him the ball. Ball in hand, he turns his back to Jimmy and Tom and walks toward the middle of the penalty area. "That's an equipment violation, and *very* reckless play, so it's going to be a Warrior penalty kick," he announces.

The Warrior bench cheers.

The crowd boos—loud enough to surprise Tom a little. Scanning the bleachers, he doesn't see any Southwind Boosters cheering, just watching the game intently. Chaz the Spaz jogs in. "It's mine," he shouts to his teammates, some of whom roll their eyes at one another.

The ref sets the ball on the penalty spot, a mere twelve yards from the goal.

A few Warriors laugh and point at Jimmy's filthy gray socks as he stands off to the side of the goal, putting on Magnus's sneakers.

"Focus, Jimmy," Tom says, trying to sound pumped.

Jimmy returns to the goal mouth, the toes of Magnus's huge sneakers flopping in the turf like swimming fins. He plants his heels on the goal line, legs at roughly shoulder width, and rolls his pants back up above his knees. Bending at the knees slightly, bouncing on the balls of his feet, he raises his hands into patty-cake position.

"Keeper, you are *not* to move until the ball is struck," the ref says. "Do you understand me?"

Jimmy nods and clenches his jaw.

"Kicker, on my whistle," the man says, nodding to the Spaz. The man sticks the whistle in his mouth with his left hand and points to the ball with his right.

"Jimmy, watch his knees, commit to one side, and dive," Tom says.

Eyes riveted on the ball, Jimmy says, simply, "Got it."

The ref blows the whistle, and Tom feels his stomach clench.

Chaz approaches the ball and strikes it, sending it just to the right of where Jimmy's standing.

Leaning in the opposite direction, Jimmy reaches back with his left hand.

The ball flicks across his fingertips and dribbles into the back of the net.

Silence.

Then a whistle.

Then a mixture of Warrior whoops from the bench and boos from the stands.

Tom jogs over to his teammates gathered around Jimmy. "That was pretty close," he says. "Not much you can do."

"Guess not," Jimmy mutters back, kicking up a clod of dirt with Magnus's Swedish clown sneakers.

Tom turns to Goatee, whose eyes dart—nervously, it

148

seems—between his cleats and the Warrior bench. Seeing Tom watching him, he takes a few steps forward, as if to join the others around Jimmy. "Good try, Jimmy," he says.

The words ring uncomfortably in Tom's ears.

Despite Tom and Yuri's encouragement, their teammates sulk back to the circle for the kickoff. As if now hyperaware of being down a goal, they play superconservative defense. Yuri directs players to feed Tom and Katya, but, now seemingly afraid to even hold the ball in their own end, the Boosters lapse into a kick-and-chase game that Tom remembers—and not fondly—from his earliest days as a player. The Boosters essentially boot the ball away every time they get it, then set up for another offensive attack. While their defense is solid, Tom notes, he also knows what happens to teams that don't actively try to score. They don't score.

And somewhere near the end of the half, the Warriors do. Greg Plutakis, back in the game for the Spaz, takes a heel pass from a Warrior striker and nails a twenty-yard blast before Yuri can slide over into defensive position.

As Tom watches the ball sail on a line drive toward the right side of the net, he knows that a more experienced goalkeeper would probably be farther into the penalty area, cutting down the angle.

Jimmy takes two flop-footed steps out from the goal mouth and dives, but he's one step short.

At halftime, the Boosters camp out next to the school building. While Katya wheels Mr. Gaz over from the sidelines, Yuri and the others pass water bottles around.

Jimmy, sullen, leans against the building. "You sure no one's got an extra pair of cleats for Jimmy?" Tom says, noting Goatee's feet and the zipped-up pack next to him. "What about you, Brad?"

Goatee looks up at him. "No," the sweeperback says. "Can't help him."

"Mind if I check and see?" Tom takes a step toward Goatee's pack.

Preston and Magnus prop themselves up on their elbows and give Tom a strange look. "Come on," Preston says. "Let's not get all tweaked. These guys are good."

"I'll show you myself," Goatee grumbles, unzipping the pack and dumping out its contents: a watch, a pair of sneakers, and that ratty Red Sox cap. "Happy?"

Tom keeps watching the kid. "It'd just be nice to have a goalkeeper with cleats—"

"I don't need any fricking cleats," Jimmy barks. "Just try to score a fricking goal once in a while."

"I will," Tom says, finally turning away from Goatee and eyeing the field. "Someone toss me a water bottle."

Katya and Mr. Gaz return, and the old man delivers his chalk-talk. Yuri and Katya both translate, but there's little new information in the old man's comments. According to him, the Boosters are, indeed, playing better soccer than they have ever played—defensively, at least. The communication has never been more constant or clearer, Stanley and Alex have finally learned to support the player with the ball, and Magnus's Swedish head completely rules the air.

But the offense . . . Mr. Gaz confirms Tom's assessment that the defense is releasing the ball too hastily, in a panicked sort of way. Simply booting the ball out of the defensive third of the field accomplishes nothing more than returning possession to the Warriors, requiring the Boosters, in turn, to set up on defense all over again, preventing them from getting any offensive attack in motion.

"So, what's the answer?" Preston says, eyes squinted as if he has just been presented with a mathematical problem.

"*Terpeniye*," Mr. Gaz says.

"Patience," Katya and Yuri translate in unison.

"He says," Katya adds, "that the defense should take at least one moment to see where the next pass might go before clearing the ball away."

Mr. Gaz rattles off something else.

Yuri translates: "Even if you put the ball to space, try to put it to a space closer to one of our players than one of their midfielders or fullbacks."

"Sounds simple enough," Preston says. "Does that make sense to you, Tom?"

Tom nods. "The trick is remembering it when you've actually got the ball on your foot."

"This guy." Yuri rests a hand on Tom's shoulder and surveys the group. "You want to put the ball on *his* foot."

Katya clears her throat and punches her brother in the shoulder.

"Or *her* foot," Yuri adds.

Tom kicks off to Katya by pushing the ball ahead the one required revolution, but she surprises him by immediately turning the ball back to Yuri, who dishes off to

Stanley at the left-wing fullback position. "*Terpeniye*—patience!" Yuri shouts as Stanley traps the ball. Stanley looks ready to boot the ball up the sideline but hesitates, dribbling back into the center a few yards and returning the ball to Yuri. Preston, seeing the striker who'd been approaching Stanley now veer toward Yuri, cuts straight across the field and calls for the diagonal pass. On the run, he traps the ball, knocks it ahead a couple yards, and releases a pass back to Blue Hair at the right-wing full-back. "Nice!" Yuri shouts. "Slow it down."

The series of short passes puts the Southwind strikers and midfielders in motion, Tom notices, so he moves into open space and calls for the ball. Blue Hair's pass is weak—a "hospital pass," the kind that both its intended receiver and a defender can reach at the same time. Tom manages to get the inside of his right foot on the ball, cutting the ball hard to his left and away from the player. He then quickly changes the ball's direction with the outside of his foot. As the kid stumbles to follow the ball, Tom feels the cleats against the back of his leg: classic Chaz the Spaz soccer.

Turning the ball downfield, he feels one more good kick at his ankles, so he passes to Paul Marcotte, all alone out at the right-wing midfield position.

"Good pressure, Chuck!" Coach Dempsey shouts from the sidelines. "Good intensity."

Katya makes a great run up the right sideline, trading places with Alex, the other striker. The switch confuses the Warrior defenders enough for Katya to settle the ball Paul sends her from the right-wing midfield. She turns it two dribbles toward the center of the field.

Tom makes a run up the center, just ten yards or so to Katya's left, and calls for the square pass—into the space dead even with her.

Katya draws her right leg back to send the ball to the space he's about to enter. The Warrior defender rushing toward her slides at her feet, but she cuts the ball in a flash back out to the sideline again, giving her an open run all the way to the right corner of the Southwind end.

Tom continues his run down the center of the field, urging Alex to keep heading left. "Stay wide!" he calls.

Katya draws Kyle Erdmann out to the corner, fakes a pass back to Paul, who has dropped in for support, then cuts again to her inside, beating Kyle and giving herself room for two quick dribbles along the goal line and a quick, chest-high pass to Tom.

Two yards away from a tangle of Warrior bodies, Tom traps the ball off his chest, turns his back to the defenders, and executes his favorite move when a mark is right on his heels: he rotates his body to the right sharply, as if to begin pushing the ball to the right with his left foot, but he steps over the ball, quickly shifting his weight back in the other direction and carrying the ball to his left with the inside of his right foot.

It works. Pushing the ball to the left, he leaves two players behind him—committed to tackles in the wrong direction. He turns to strike the ball on goal, but when he glances up at the defense he finds Alex directly in his line.

"Heel!" Yuri shouts.

Without looking, Tom heels the ball back, aiming with his ears to a spot of grass he can't see.

He's only half-turned when he sees the ball fly in a

line-drive blur of white out to the right side of the penalty area. In three lightning fast but distinct motions, Katya jumps into the air, bends her torso back, and snaps forward like a cobra striking. The ball rockets off her head and into the upper-right corner of the Warrior net.

For a second, Tom doesn't cheer, feeling more like he has just watched a soccer camp videotape than actually experienced something real. The whole sequence, minus Alex's field position, was soccer camp–video perfect.

As the Boosters mob Katya and Yuri, Tom turns to Brad Goatee, catching the kid looking toward the Southwind bench. A few seconds later, seeing Tom watching him, Goatee pumps his fist and cheers. *Kind of a lame cheer*, Tom thinks.

Tom feels someone grab him around the shoulders from behind, and he turns to find Alex beaming at him. "Sorry I got in your way," he says, drooling a little with glee.

"No problem," Tom says. "Just keep moving to space. Play the whole field."

Tom meets up with Katya just outside the center circle and gives her a hug as the Warriors set up for another kickoff. "Nice finish," he says. "Like something you'd see on television."

"I actually scored like this once on Moscow television," Katya says, bending to pull up her socks.

"Well, see if you can do it a couple more times."

The whistle blows, and the Warriors kick off. The Boosters lapse back briefly into their conservative defense, especially Magnus and Yuri, who direct the others to shift around, adjusting for the Warrior advances—advances that don't blow Tom away with their strategic brilliance.

Exactly the opposite. Chaz is as spastic a center middie as he has ever seen, booting the ball as impulsively as the most desperate sweeperback. He's hardly a playmaker.

At almost the exact instant Tom makes this assessment, Dempsey subs Greg Plutakis back in for the Spaz. Chaz swears, whines, and kicks up dirt all the way back to the bench.

Tom and Yuri look at each other, silently concurring, as Plutakis takes the field, that the Boosters are indeed giving the Warriors an honest match. Tom had taken Chaz's entry into the game as a slight: this was how seriously Dempsey was taking this contest—Chuckie-Dempsey-at-center-midfield serious. Seeing him yanked from the match tells Tom the Warriors are officially about to try their hardest.

The Boosters settle back into their game. It takes only Blue Hair's one mindless boot of the ball out of the Boosters' end, and a *"terpeniye*—patience!" reminder from Yuri, to get the fullbacks and midfielders moving the ball around among one another, pulling the Warrior defense apart, creating opportunities to send the ball up to Katya and Tom.

The Booster middies and backs play steady, solid soccer, losing the nervous energy that had unraveled them in the first half. They win tackles, they lose tackles, but they talk through it all. Most impressively, to Tom, they are patient in the way they move the ball out of their defensive end.

The true genius of the team's field formation hits Tom about midway through the second half, when he and Katya settle into a kind of offensive rhythm: virtually each Warrior advance results in a turnover in the Boosters' defensive third, a fullback pass to the middies, and a pass up to Katya or Tom, less often to Alex. If Tom gets the ball, he carries until the first real defender comes on, then executes a give-and-go with Katya—passing to her and running past his defender to receive a pass back from her on the other side of the man. If Katya gets the pass, Tom does the same, encouraging Alex to run into open space down in the Southwind end but taking care not to run too far and get caught behind the last defender: offsides.

Katya is a freestyle striker, Tom observes with a touch of frustration. Although he runs to support her wherever she goes, she seems intent on trying to beat defenders until it's absolutely clear that she can't. It's a kind of play Tom doesn't like—too risky, too vulnerable to quick turnovers against fullbacks who can send the ball, with one good boot, back into the Boosters' offensive territory.

The moment the concern strikes Tom, he notices that Goatee has wandered much farther into the Southwind defensive third than a sweeperback would ordinarily venture on a throw-in. "Brad," Tom calls, "step back. If they clear it, you're caught too far up."

Goatee nods and jogs back a few yards.

Tom watches him, catching the kid shoot a quick glance at the Warrior bench.

Just as Tom had predicted, Kyle Erdmann, the Warrior sweeper, picks up the throw-in and clears it past the midfield. Magnus takes the ball out of the air and heads it to Yuri, who settles the ball, looks upfield, then turns and sends a crisp rolling pass back to Goatee. "Patience," Yuri shouts. "Midfielders, support or move to—"

In executing a simple trap, Goatee leaves his foot too

high, allowing the ball to slip underneath and toward the goal.

Tom watches the sweeperback slowly turn around as two Warrior strikers descend on the ball from both sides. By the time Goatee has turned, the Warrior center striker already has the ball, leaving Goatee—no speed demon—a good step behind. The wing striker runs past the ball, setting up a give-and-go.

Yuri and Magnus sprint straight back into the penalty area, Yuri after the ball handler, Magnus to the supporting striker. As the center dishes off to his wing, Magnus is just a half step away, creating a hospital pass. The wing makes the trap but, under pressure from Magnus, passes the ball ahead to the center striker making a run for the goal—Yuri dogging him every step.

As the center striker pulls a step ahead of Yuri, Jimmy bolts out of the goal. He slides along the grass just as the striker is cocking his right leg. When the kid takes the shot, Jimmy already has his left arm over the ball. The shot goes straight into his chest, and as he rolls to cover the ball, he takes the striker's legs out from under him. Yuri and a Warrior midfielder trip on the arms and legs sticking out from the pile.

"Aaarrrgh!" Jimmy screams, rolling away from the heap. He grabs his right foot and rocks onto his back, muttering, "Frick, frick, frick, frick . . ."

The ref blows the whistle.

"You okay, Jimmy?" Preston says, crouching beside him.

"I'll be okay," Jimmy snarls through his teeth, his face twisted in a grimace.

"You stub your toe?" Preston says.

"Someone stubbed it for me."

"Do you think it's broken?"

"Nah." Jimmy stands and walks around in a circle, limping and hopping on one foot. "Just give me a second."

Tom turns to the bleachers, spotting his mother standing up and looking toward him.

Catching Tom's eye, she gestures with her hands out to her sides, as if to ask if she should come down onto the field.

Tom turns back to Jimmy, who's walking more normally now but still grumbling, "Frick, frick, frick." Turning back to his mother, Tom shakes his head.

She sits back down.

"We'll give you a minute, keeper," the ref says as Jimmy hobbles back into the goal mouth, "then we need to keep going."

"How much time do we have left?" Tom asks the ref.

The man checks his watch. "About ten minutes."

"One for each toe," a Warrior midfielder says, drawing laughter from a couple of his teammates.

Tom glares at them but a second later notices Goatee standing off by himself, staring at the ground inside the penalty area roughly where the collision occurred. Tom walks over to him. "You need to settle down, Brad," he says.

Goatee looks up at him with alarm, as if Tom has caught him in some illegal act. "I'm going to," he says.

"Well, don't waste time thinking about it. Just do it."

Goatee narrows his eyes at him.

Tom glares back.

When Goatee starts to look away, Tom flicks a hand against his shoulder. "The game's over here. I mean, tell me you know *that* much about soccer—"

"I know how to play soccer," Goatee snaps.

"Then why do you keep looking over at the bench?"

Goatee looks down at his cleats.

"You have some deal going with Dempsey?" Tom says.

Goatee says nothing.

"That's what it is, isn't it?"

Goatee turns away, but Tom leans so he's in his field of vision. "Did the guy promise you a starting spot if you help us lose? Is that it?"

"No."

"Then what is it, Brad?"

Goatee is silent again, and as he stares at the ground, Tom scans the Warriors bench.

Tom watches Dempsey talking to two players—Greg Plutakis and the British kid. The coach rests one hand on each of his players' shoulders as he talks. Tom recalls his conversations with Dempsey, how the man always succeeded in getting him too amped up to think clearly.

"I'll tell you what, Brad," Tom says, "that guy is really manipulative. I wouldn't blame you if you got suckered into something—"

"It was Chaz," Goatee blurts out. He looks at Tom with wide eyes, as if challenging him to deny it.

"What?"

"Yeah. Chaz told me to do it. He told me to make sure you guys lose."

"What? Why would you do something like—"

159

"He said his father told him to tell me to do it."

Tom looks over at the Southwind bench again, where Dempsey is standing, arms crossed, looking in Tom's direction.

"He said if I made sure you guys lost, he wouldn't cut me from the team," Goatee adds, ending with a bitter-sounding laugh and a shake of his head.

Still watching Dempsey, Tom replays in his mind the previous night's conversation with him at the Nucleus, how the man had been tough at first but became more reasonable, only to throw down his secret weapon—the deal about playing full field, full sides. But before that, Tom recalls, he'd spoken of his Vietnam buddies, and of honor, and of something more than just tradition for tradition's sake. And he'd actually seemed to mean it.

Though Tom knows that in this very instant he could also be letting himself get suckered into another one of Dempsey's traps, he at least considers the possibility that maybe there really is a reasonable man buried somewhere inside all that stubborn Warrior pride. "No," Tom says. "I don't think it's the coach. He's hardheaded, for sure, but . . ." He turns to Brad. "This kind of scam is too low even for him."

Goatee finally looks up and glares at the Warrior bench. "You're probably right," he says, shaking his head. "It probably was just Chaz—"

"Of course it was. You want to know why?"

"Because I'm stupid—"

"No. Because you're a better player than he is."

Goatee looks at Tom but doesn't seem to know what to say.

"Chaz is pretty sneaky," Tom adds, "but we'd play one against eleven with these guys before we'd let him on our team."

"I'm sorry," Brad says. "I didn't think the scrimmage would get like this."

"Neither did Dempsey." Tom gestures to Greg Plutakis. "Chaz is back on the bench. The starters are all in."

Passing Tom and Goatee, the ref blows the whistle practically in Tom's ear. "We're going to have a goal kick," he shouts, tossing the ball to Brad.

Tom takes the ball from the sweeperback's hands. "Tell me, Brad, do we have *our* best team out?"

Brad looks around the field, noticing his teammates taking up positions, Jimmy bouncing on the balls of his feet in the goalie box. "What are we called again? Like, what's our team name?"

"Doesn't matter." Tom tosses him the ball. "Boot this thing a mile. Pretend it's Chaz's butt."

Goatee puts the ball back in play at the midfield, and the Boosters pick up where they left off, moving the ball around patiently and a degree more crisply than before. They make runs to open spaces but hustle back to play conservative defense.

The Warrior strikers, maybe sensing a weakened goalie in the net, also come alive, stringing together more short passes in the Boosters' end, firing more shots on goal, most from outside the penalty area, thanks to Yuri's, Magnus's, and now Goatee's coordination of the defense.

All in all, the teams play evenly but without much serious offensive action. Even the crowd seems to quiet down a little as Tom and Katya fail to penetrate very far into the

Southwind end. Growing antsy, Tom decides to abandon the short-passing give-and-go with Katya and instead carry the ball as far as he can.

A few plays later, Yuri steals the ball from Greg Plutakis and dishes off to Tom. Tom fakes a onetime pass to Katya in the center and cuts toward the right sideline, beating a Southwind midfielder easily. A few yards down the line, he cuts back toward the center. As the Southwind stopper approaches, he executes his second-favorite move, a variation on his favorite: He shifts his body to the left and sweeps his right leg to the left, as if to cut the ball hard in that direction. But he sweeps his right foot over the ball and, a split second later, knocks it to the right with the outside of his right foot. While the defender's body is leaning in the opposite direction, Tom shifts course back toward the sideline, picking up an easy ten more yards.

A wing fullback barrels straight at him, moving at full speed. Tom uses the kid's intensity to his advantage, slowing the ball and timing a little push of the ball right through the defender's legs—a move he has always known as a "nutmeg," though no one has ever been able to explain why it's called that.

Cutting the ball toward the center again, he sees Kyle Erdmann stepping up to mark him. By now, he can also hear Greg Plutakis right on his heels. As Kyle makes his move, his head lowered like a bull charging a matador, Tom spots Katya in his peripheral vision, shuffling off to his left. Before he can even turn to her, she sprints behind Kyle and toward the empty space to his right. Tom takes a step to the left and, just before Kyle and Plutakis squeeze him from both sides, dishes the ball to the empty space.

162

Watching Katya meet the ball, Tom takes two more steps to the left, pulling his defenders with him. Without looking back, Katya heels the ball to the spot he's just left. Tom digs his cleats into the ground and starts to turn. Eyeing the ball on its way to no one, he sees a blur of Yuri flash in front of him, hears the unmistakable contact of leather on leather, sees the Russian leap into his follow-through like a fox clearing bushes by the side of a road . . .

. . . the ripple of net . . .

. . . and an explosion of cheers from the stands—louder, it seems to Tom, than before.

Tom looks into the bleachers and finds even a few Southwind Boosters clapping their hands—politely, though, as if they're at a piano recital, not a soccer match.

The game is tied.

After getting momentarily mobbed by his teammates, Tom and the others jog back to the center circle for the Warrior kickoff. He's puzzled to see Chaz Dempsey coming back onto the field, though to replace a wing midfielder, not Greg Plutakis. As he crosses in front of Tom, Chaz mutters, "She's pretty good, Tom, your little squaw."

Tom glowers at him but can't think of anything to say.

"No, buddy, you're the great player, *eh-ctually,*" Katya says, pulling up alongside Chaz. "You have all that room for your penalty kick, but you still manage to hit the ball off our goalkeeper. *Deadly* accuracy, buddy." She follows Chaz a few yards, staring him down.

Chaz, seemingly challenged to summon a comeback, just sneers at Katya, mutters "Commie," and veers away.

"Anarchist, *eh-ctually,*" Katya says, winking at Tom.

The Warriors kick off and immediately reveal their plan for the remaining minutes of the game: aggressive, physical play. On their first couple of offensive pushes, Tom notices the Warrior midfielders shoving at their marks, which seems more like football pass coverage than soccer defense. Preston ends up right on his butt after one good shove from the Spaz while the ref is looking elsewhere, even though neither of them was anywhere near the ball. From down on the ground, Preston glares at the ref, who obviously missed the foul. Tom begins jogging toward his teammate to intervene in case Preston decides to address the ref—and earn the red card, and the ejection from the match, that the team simply can't afford. To Tom's amazement, Preston says nothing.

On defense, the physical contact is just as aggressive. During each give-and-go with Katya, Tom feels the cleats scraping his shins and ankles.

It's worse for Katya, though. Seeing Chaz block her with his shoulder, even after she has passed the ball, makes Tom almost not want to pass to her. This, he understands, is probably part of the Southwind strategy. Kyle Erdmann is no less delicate with her, knocking her over twice without making any ball contact.

Again, the ref's attention is elsewhere.

"Intensity!" Coach Dempsey shouts as Tom is running past the Warrior bench. A second later, he sees Alex blatantly yanked off the ball by his shirttail. As he topples onto the grass, the ref blows the whistle and awards the Boosters a free kick. Tom begins to wonder, as he jogs into position, if the word *intensity* is Dempsey's secret code for *"Take someone out!"*

During the brief break in the action, as the ref paces a few Warriors back ten yards from the ball for the Boosters' free kick, Tom notices the Spaz talking to Katya, following her step for step. He can't hear what Chaz is saying, but he can guess. He starts to jog over, but Katya looks up at him and shakes her head, gestures for him to stay out of it. A moment later, the ball is back in play.

The game degrades rapidly, with Warriors pushing and shoving and tripping Boosters all over the field every time the ref isn't looking. Spectators begin to boo the infractions, and once or twice Tom sees even a few Southwind Athletic Boosters on their feet, complaining about something the ref has missed. The whole energy of the match seems to be transforming, Tom thinks, just as the sky has grown darker. Jogging past the Warrior bench, he hears a string of racial slurs he hasn't heard since he was a very small boy. Coach Dempsey doesn't chime in, but he doesn't silence his players either.

Tom catches his mother's eye. She's watching him, perched on the edge of her seat, hands clasped in front of her in that way she holds them when she's anxious about something.

Gazing downfield, Tom sees Brad Goatee settle the ball out at the right wing.

Two Southwind players—a wing striker and a wing midfielder—approach Brad, one moving in for a tackle, the other running to an open space a few yards away, as if Brad might hit him with a pass there, even though he's on the opposing team. Goatee shifts his body weight as if to pass but fakes it, rolling the ball with the bottom of his cleat, then pulling it back in the other direction. With the striker leaning in the wrong direction, Goatee cuts the ball to the sideline and, glancing up at Tom, sends him a long, perfect pass.

As if on instinct now, Tom turns the ball toward the center and hits Katya for the give-and-go. As he's moving to collect her return pass, however, Chaz slides into her from behind, buckling her at the knees and sending her flying face-down onto the grass.

"Oh, come on, ref!" Tom shouts.

The crowd erupts in boos. Even the Southwind Athletic Boosters—almost every single one of them—stomp their feet on the bleachers in protest.

The referee blows his whistle, but as soon as the whistle falls from his mouth, he reaches into his shirt pocket and brandishes the yellow card at Tom. "You know better than to speak to the officials that way, son," the man not so much says as declares, like a judge reading a sentence. With the crowd booing even more loudly now, the ref tucks the yellow card back into his pocket, pulls out the red, and, holding it above his head like a magician doing a card trick, walks it over to Chaz.

The crowd cheers as Chaz makes an outraged face, begins to approach the ref, and is finally called off the field by his father.

Tom jogs over to Katya, who writhes in pain, clutching her knees to her chest, Yuri already at her side.

"We have an injury, sir," Yuri says to the ref, barely masking his disgust. "Can we have a few minutes?"

The ref looks to the sideline and shouts, "Time!"

"How much time is left?" Preston asks, passing the ref on his way to Katya's side.

The ref looks at his watch. "Just under two minutes."

Tom turns to the stands to beckon his mother, but she's already crossing the field at a jog. Reaching Katya, she gently straightens her knees out and begins asking her questions.

Out of the corner of his eye, Tom sees the Spaz heading toward the bench. Halfway there, a teammate tosses him a water bottle. Another kid coming off the sideline gives him a low five, down at the waist. While Chaz sucks on a water bottle, Tom approaches him.

"Nice 'intensity,' Chuckie. Enjoy that bench ride—"

"Wahoo," the Spaz spits.

For a split second, Tom feels like plowing the Spaz right over the bench and pummeling him into the ground, but, remembering the ref's yellow card waving in front of his face, he walks in a little circle, restraining himself. Instead, he turns to Dempsey. "Hey, Coach," he says, "your son turned out to be quite a warrior. Yeah, he's real brave."

Dempsey doesn't say anything right away. Tiny dots of rain begin collecting on the pink dome of his head.

"You've got yourself a team, there, Tom," the man finally says. "I'll give you that."

"You're not giving us anything. We're fighting for it. *We're* the warriors. And we're going to beat you in the overtime."

Dempsey just stares, his jaw working frantically on his chewing gum. As the raindrops begin tapping a rhythm on the grass, something seems to register in his stolid gaze.

His eyebrows spike once, and he holds one hand open, palm to the sky. "There's not going to be an overtime," he says. "Seems we've got a rain coming on. I don't want the pitch all torn up for the season opener."

"We have to play overtime," Tom says. "We agreed to a match."

"Absolutely. And we're playing our match. And it's been a good match—"

"We had a deal."

Coach Dempsey looks over Tom's shoulder, and the applause from the stands tells Tom that Katya is on her feet again. As he turns toward her, however, he sees Preston and Yuri helping her off the field, his mother walking two steps ahead.

"Probably just a sprain," Tom's mother says to him, giving his hand a squeeze as she passes. "But I'm going to bring her in for an x-ray."

As Tom watches them carry Katya away, the ref draws alongside Tom and Coach Dempsey. "What are we doing, Coach?" he says.

Dempsey approaches Tom, his eyes squinting in the quickening drizzle. "You're down to ten players," he says. "You don't stand a chance in the overtime."

"Let's play it and see—"

"Call the game right here, Tom," Dempsey goes on. "A draw. And my last offer stands. Walk on next week with Southwind, walk off whenever you want."

Tom looks to the sideline, where two Southwind Athletic Boosters are now taking Katya from Yuri and Preston, who turn back to the field. "I'm just one player on this team," he says. "And we're all equals. And we're finishing the match."

"Think about what you're doing, kid. You play these next two minutes . . ."—Dempsey laughs to himself, as if baffled by Tom's stupidity—"and you never, *ever* wear a Warriors jersey. Oh, you think you can handle that now, but wait till school starts. New kid, new school. Practically the only Mohawk. You'll be nobody."

Tom looks into the stands, where the spectators are all on their feet, some with makeshift newspaper umbrellas opened over their heads. He looks down toward the Boosters goal, where Magnus is jumping up and down, rocking his head from side to side, staying limber. Beyond the goal, his mother is helping Katya into the back seat of their car.

His father materializes at the corner then, hands clasped behind his back, eyes closed, a tranquil face aimed skyward as if to wash himself in the rain.

"Lighten up, Coach," Tom says, feeling the strangest urge to laugh. "It's just a game."

"Don't test me," Dempsey says with a sneer. "Play these two minutes, and—win or lose—you get nothing."

"Not even if we win?"

"Dream on," Dempsey says.

"So your word is no good?"

Dempsey snorts. "I don't make deals with hotshots."

Tom feels someone poking him in the back. He whirls around.

Jimmy.

"I don't know what you fricking guys are talking

169

about," Jimmy says, "but we're finishing this match, even if the ref makes me wear someone's fricking pants next. That'll give you a chance to kiss my butt, Coach."

"You realize I'm the athletic director of this school," Dempsey hisses.

"Another argument for homeschooling." Jimmy jogs back to the goal.

Tom turns to the ref. "We play," he says, walking away.

"Armand, we're going to play out the clock," Dempsey adds, nodding to the ref, "but no OT."

The ref sets the ball down more or less where he'd issued Chaz the red card.

"Nothing, Tom!" Dempsey calls to him.

Tom ignores him.

A couple of seconds later, the crowd begins chanting "Boo-*sters,* Boo-*sters,* Boo-*sters* . . ." The sound seems almost too loud to be coming from just one hundred or so people. There's a faint background sound enveloping the cheers—a white noise . . . like static . . .

"It's going to be a Boosters direct kick," the ref shouts and blows his whistle.

The whistle shriek is practically swallowed up in the drumming of rain and a strange . . . roar.

As Tom watches Yuri knock the ball into play, he experiences the sensation that he has watched it all before, on TV somewhere, during some Raven chalk-talk, in his dreams. He hardly moves an inch, as if knowing that Alex will blow the trap but that the Warrior middie will fail to control the ball tightly enough, allowing Preston to scoop it up and dish a nice square pass to Yuri. Even when Yuri sends the ball sizzling along the glistening grass toward

170

him, Tom not so much takes the pass as *witnesses* himself taking the pass, as if he's making the play and watching from the bleachers at the same time.

The roar blocks out all sound except for his breathing— his breathing and the clicking of rain, like iron chips falling from a skyscraper hidden in the clouds. Tom moves, seemingly in slow motion, across the center of the field.

He hits Paul making a run for the right corner of the Southwind end, marveling, as he bolts up the center of the field, at the architecture of the game—the ball cutting lines, angles, arcs; the players rushing to weld connections in place before sending the ball across the structure.

Paul catches up to the ball just before it rolls over the Warrior goal line and turns it back two yards.

Tom slides into a spot just outside the penalty area and watches Paul fire a beautiful cross-field pass to Alex— camped out on the left side of the field, staying out wide for a change. Tom calls for the ball.

Alex takes the pass off his chest, settles it with his right foot, cuts the ball to his inside, quickly to his outside, then back to his inside, beating his defender and giving himself an opportunity to send a perfect, chest-high cross out to Tom at the top of the box.

Preston suddenly blocks Tom's view of the ball as he runs directly in its arcing path.

As if focusing each eye on something different, Tom watches Preston's move pull two Warrior defenders to the left, out of the way, leaving Tom an open, straight look at the goal, with a little more than a yard of space on each side of the Warrior goalkeeper.

Tom moves on impulse: two steps to the line at the top of the penalty area, a leap, a lean to the right, a scissors-cutting motion with his right leg as his body falls parallel, right shoulder to the ground, like a metal beam being dropped onto the field.

The ball connects with his left instep in that spot where they were destined to meet.

He tries to watch the shot but closes his eyes as his right shoulder and chest hit the ground. He rolls once, eyes still closed, a smile on his face, as if playfully resisting hands trying to tuck him into bed. The cheering explodes like thunder all around him . . .

"Kawehras—'the thunder.'"

Or is it laughter he hears echoing deep inside his head, as if through time?

He feels as if he could sleep, the bodies falling on top of him now like the "Indian" blankets his father kept in the trunk of his car. He kept two back there, in case he and Tom ever got stuck somewhere. In case they had no choice but to wait out a storm.